Pretty Little Dead Girls

A Novel of Murder and Whimsy

Mercedes M. Yardley

Crystal Lake Publishing
www.CrystalLakePub.com

To the Simply Tims, Rikki-Tikkis,
Detective Bridgers, and other beautiful
warriors of the world.

Link arms and stand up for all of us.

Chapter One
A Body is Found

Bryony Adams was the type of girl who got murdered.

This was always so, and it was apparent from the way men looked at her as she adjusted her knee socks, to the way women shook their heads in pity when she rode by on her bicycle.

"I made you a present, Mrs. Lopez," she said, dragging her backpack over to the desk. A vivid orange poster hung on the wall, demonstrating how to tie shoes. Bryony was well versed in tying her shoes, and could even double knot, but that was because she and her father worked very, very hard on it at home. Now she was working on counting to one hundred and was almost there, although sometimes she got lost while wandering around in the ever elusive eighties.

"Oh, did you? What a sweet girl you are. What did you make?"

Bryony pulled the gift out of the backpack, and set it on the desk. A bookmark, made of bright construction paper with cheap sequins glued to it. A cockeyed Mrs. Lopez was painstakingly drawn in crayon, her smile extending beyond the circle of her face. She had purple hair and a star sitting on one shoulder. Mrs. Lopez's eyes stung. She clutched the girl to her, and as she felt the thin bones and coltish knees, she thought, *Run away, little girl. Run from everything that is going to befall you. Just run, Bryony. Run.*

What she said out loud was, "It's very beautiful, Bryony. I have a special fondness for purple sequins, too."

Kindergarten did not kill her.

Mrs. Lopez cried as Bryony pranced across the school's tiny stage to receive her diploma. She hugged her teacher and gravely shook the hand of the principal, and then waved wildly to her father who sat in the second row.

"She's yours now," Mrs. Lopez whispered to Mr. Egan, the first grade teacher. "Watch over her, Larry. Keep her safe."

"Oh heavens, that little girl is going to die in my care," Mr. Egan muttered back.

As soon as the kindergarten graduation ended, he went directly home to pour himself a drink, and then several drinks. When he awoke the following morning, with a pounding head and heavy tongue, he decided then and there that he wouldn't drink again. He needed his wits about him if he was going to help the Star Girl live.

And live she did, all through the first grade.

She painted ceramic ducks for a class project and watched baby chicks hatch for Easter, and lost her first tooth without mishap.

"Thank you for being my teacher," Bryony said to Mr. Egan on the last day of school. "I enjoyed this class so very much."

"It was a pleasure," he answered honestly, and breathed a sigh of relief and trepidation. Although she had not been murdered nor even really threatened that year, not once, it only meant she was prolonging the inevitable. Surely the time was nearing.

When Bryony was in the second grade, a tiny body was found half buried under the desert sand. The coyotes had gotten to her, but not too badly, thanks to Patty Farlan. Patty, the high school druggie ringleader, was out partying with his friends nearby, and the bonfire scared the animals off. Patty and his flavor-of-the-week girlfriend, whose name nobody cared about or would remember, least of all Patty, stumbled across her.

"Patty," said Flavor, "will you love me forever? Really, true?"

"Sure, sure," said Patty, and then, "Oh my (these words shall be forever censored) what the (censor censor) is that?! It looks like a (censor) body out in the (censored for the sake of children) desert!"

It took a while for everybody at the party to sober up and come down, and after they did, Patty gave the police a call.

"Hey, man. There's a body out in the desert. I found it when I was, uh, studying the desert nightlife, man. I think . . . I think it's a little girl."

Immediately the receptionist thought of Bryony. Poor girl, it had happened. It was time. She snuffled a little and pressed the magic red button on the station's telephone.

"What?" said the voice on the receiver.

"Tim," she said. Not Mr. Tim or Captain Tim or any of the other formal titles that he had garnished in his illustrious career. No, they were small town born and small town raised, and Tim was Tim. Thirty years from now when Tim would become President of the United States, he would shirk at being called President Lowry, but he would do it for the good of the country, dragging his feet all the while. But for here and now, he is Tim, and Tim is who he is, and being Simply Tim is good enough for everybody.

"Tim," she said, "Patty is on the line."

"Is he seeing dragons at the grocery store again?"

"No, he said that he was out in the desert looking at the animals," (there was a barely audible snort from Tim, but his restraint can only be admired) "and he came across . . . well, Tim, Patty says that he found a body."

"A body?" Tim snapped to full attention.

The receptionist took a deep breath. "A . . . little girl, he says."

There was silence, and then Tim said, "Has anybody contacted Bryony's father yet?"

"Of course not. The call just barely came in."

Simply Tim was already pulling his jacket over his stooped shoulders. They were not stooped a moment ago, but suddenly the air above them weighed more than he could bear. "Get the crew. I'll check in on Stop Adams when we know more. Heaven knows that man has been dreading this visit all of his life. Poor Stop. Poor Bryony, rest her pretty little soul."

The Sergeant and his crew somberly made the drive out to the desert.

The coyotes howled in sorrow over their loss.

Heavy boots crunched over frozen sand, now thawing in the tentative light of morning.

There she was, tiny fingers curled, slightly bloodied at the tips. Her left arm, shoulder, and head stuck out of the ground, while the rest lay quietly beneath. They took pictures, carefully brushing the sand free.

The girl was much too big to be Bryony. The areas behind her knees were pillowy, and she had dimples at her elbows. The bruises across her face darkened her eyes like drugstore shadow, making her look years older.

"Samantha Collins," the deputy said to Tim. The shock had straightened his voice out, erasing the freewheeling cadence that he usually exhibited. The deputy's oldest girl often babysat for the Collins family. Stocked fridge, cable, well-behaved kids, she said. They paid well but not exorbitantly. Nice, middle class people.

"Huh. Who would have thought?" said Tim, rubbing his face. "She doesn't seem to be the type."

He wasn't quite sure if the deputy would understand what he meant, but the deputy nodded earnestly. "I know what you mean, Tim. Who would have thought that somebody would kill Samantha?" After all, Bryony lived just around the corner.

Samantha was buried in a simple pink casket with very little ceremony. A sweet girl, a quiet girl. A devastatingly average and unmemorable girl. The town came out and sat through the mundane, unimaginative funeral.

"That was . . . inspiring," a woman in black commented halfheartedly. This, of course, made her a liar, but it was a gentle lie with sweet intentions, and she was forgiven, nay, raised in the general esteem because of it.

"Yes," said her sister. "It was very . . . appropriate."

Indeed, it was. Appropriate and perfectly suitable. In the best of taste; a quiet, humdrum type of funeral for an obedient daughter. No scandal at all except for the shocking fact of her murder. The "Who?" and "Why?" of it didn't even come close to the real question that was on everybody's mind: "Why not Bryony?"

In fact, the only emotion that anybody really felt at the funeral was a quick, deviously delicious thrill that occurred beforehand as family and friends filed past to look at the body. Samantha was quite lovely, as luck would have it, painted and powdered and hardly looking murdered at all. Her limbs had snapped back into place wonderfully, the punctures and black bruising covered artfully with clothes and makeup.

Bryony paused by the small casket longer than was custom, and the people behind her began to feel ill at ease for her, this strange, almost mystical girl who dared throw off the flow of the viewing line. Bryony studied Samantha carefully, delicately moving away the ruffled collar to see the thin wound that ran all the way around her throat.

Bryony leaned with her face uncomfortably close to that of the corpse, who was not a corpse at all to Bryony, but her dear friend Samantha. And then she said what ears pricked to hear her say, the words that coursed like wildfire through the funeral crowd and down phone lines mere seconds after she uttered them.

"Sam, I'm sorry," she said. "I don't know what happened. It should have been me."

Nobody, not one person, soothed the bitter tears of that guilty child. Not a word was spoken, not a hand ran down her pale hair or patted her bony back comfortingly.

Because she was right. They knew it and now she knew it, and nobody else understood what had happened, either. Somebody made a mistake. Somebody had taken the wrong child.

Chapter Two
Bryony's First Kiss

So Bryony lived.

She lived past second grade and third and fourth. In fifth there was a bit of nastiness when a car swerved onto the sidewalk and nearly hit her while she was roller skating, but a thirteen year old boy zipped by on his skateboard and pushed her into the neighbor's roses. It saved her life, but scratched her up terribly, and Bryony refused to talk to him for the next three years. When he was sixteen and she was thirteen, she realized with starry eyes that he had been her hero. When he was seventeen and she was fourteen, she wrote biting notes to his girlfriend that she never sent. When he was eighteen and she was fifteen, he joined the military and was killed that very year. Bryony once again felt the fangs of death striking at her ankles, pricking her skin but not wounding her directly. It was a warning, like everything else was a warning. She knew that she would die in high school.

How does this knowledge affect a young girl? How does it change her existence, knowing that the cruel universe is hovering ever at hand, waiting to snuff out her life?

Something inside of her tender heart gave up and died, even while something else struggled to survive. Relationships and memories passively floated past her like flotsam in the tide pool while a part of her grabbed at everything desperately, pulling it to her bosom while she still had time.

Take Teddy Baker.

While her Skateboard Hero was busy not focusing his attention on her, Bryony became enamored with a rather pretty boy who was in her Music Theory class. Large brown eyes, black hair, and a somewhat melancholy countenance convinced her that he needed bounteous amounts of love to be happy, more than any one person could give, but if everybody just dropped tiny drops of love into his empty bucket of a heart, then surely one day it would fill up. Love is sometimes a collaborative effort, you see.

Bryony and Teddy both stayed after class one day, this momentous occasion marked by the ringing of the school bell. The other students and the teacher quickly abandoned the room, and Bryony twirled her light hair self-consciously around her finger while Teddy talked about his family. His woes. The struggles that he went through, the way that he was misunderstood.

"I think that people don't love you enough," Bryony said simply. Teddy blinked his rather vacant eyes, and quickly agreed.

"You're so right, Bry," he said. "Nobody loves me. Nobody really gets me at all. It's lonely sometimes, you know?"

He eyed her, gauging her reaction. Her skin was

soft and she had that otherworldly ambiance that clung to her. She slid through school as if her death had come and she was a ghost, one foot tethered on earth and the other already off in the stars. Teddy dug that. It made everything easier. It made it not quite so bad, this thing that he was about to do.

"Well, I love you," she said. Her cheeks pinked. "I mean, not like that, of course. I don't know you that well yet. But I have this theory, right? We all have a bucket. This big, empty bucket that's just waiting for somebody to fill it, and . . . "

Teddy didn't care much about big, empty buckets. He took her head in his hands, zeroed in, and pushed his mouth against hers. She kept talking for a few seconds, and finally fell silent. Teddy moved his lips a little bit like his sister instructed him to do, and he felt Bryony tentatively do something similar. Teddy pulled away and looked at her, trying to read the unusual expression on her face.

Part of her brain said, "Stop, Bryony! You are a dead girl, and you cannot get attached to anybody. One day you are going to leave suddenly and without warning, and how cruel would that be? To all of you?" That part shook its fist angrily.

The other part of her brain said, "Listen up, you, this may very well be the night. The night that has always been coming, the night when you finally sigh and your ribs still. Don't you dare miss this momentary chance at happiness!"

"Wh-what are you thinking about?" Teddy asked nervously. He hadn't had many kisses, but never in all of the movies he had watched had the kissee stared at the kisser with such concentration afterwards. It unnerved him, and rightfully so, for being judged harshly after sharing a first kiss with somebody is a horrid, horrid thing indeed.

Bryony came to a decision. "Teddy, I think that you are very sweet. If tonight is the night that I am murdered, I want to think about your eyes and the way that your hair is falling into them. I want to think about this kiss right now, because it is the first one that I have ever had. And I would like to try it again so that it is a little bit better, if that's okay with you. I wasn't really prepared."

For a second, Teddy caught a glimpse of Bryony as a little girl, when she would stare at the sky, and the clouds would pass over her eyes. She stood as tall as she could, but something was already breaking inside, and Teddy could almost hear it. The gears of her soul grinding to a halt. The bright metal filings of it struck sparks and shone like stars.

She watched him carefully, and Teddy only nodded. He pressed his lips to hers more gently this time, and it was as a first kiss should be—gentle and hopeful and full of nervous delight. He didn't invite her out as he had first planned. He didn't take her to the mesa where their headlights would sweep over the desert, where the night would reflect back eyes that couldn't be seen otherwise. He only told his friends that she refused to come, that she wanted nothing to do with him, and they would have no use for their rope and lighters and eagerly sharpened knives that night. They would have to find somebody else to practice on, somebody else to assuage their burgeoning hunger, because Bryony was on to them, he said, and would never come. Never, so don't even try.

They said hateful words about her, that devil girl who mysteriously knew so much. Teddy agreed with them, and told them that he would never talk to her again. When her gray eyes searched him out, he avoided them. Eventually they dropped to the ground whenever she saw him, and he felt her spirit crushing underneath his sneakers as he walked by. It was easy to ignore her, to even tease her when he was with his friends. But when he was by himself, it was different.

He treasured that kiss up in his heart, taking it out to test it from time to time. It always held up. It always shone.

Chapter Three
It Comes

*I*t is time.
It is time.
She always knew this day would come.

Chapter Four
Defy the Desert

*B*ryony gave her father a kiss on his withered cheek.

"I can't live here anymore, daddy. The desert is calling out for my bones. Do you understand that?"

Of course Stop Adams understood it. He'd known it for years, ever since she was a baby, practically. His wife had tried to tell him since the day Bryony was born, but he never listened. Finally she had packed up.

"I can't stand here waiting for my little girl to die, Stop. I can't take it one more minute. One more second. I will always love you, and her." She kissed them both on the cheek, just as Bryony kissed him now.

They both said the same words.

"I can't live here anymore."

"I understand, baby girl," Stop said.

His heart quietly broke in half, but he knew that he would shuffle home and sew it back together again. Old men break and break and break into smaller pieces, going on until there is nothing left. He always had something left, as long as he had his daughter. He knew that on the day she died, he would disappear, as well, and they would rejoice together wherever it was they would rejoice. But until then, he stayed. He didn't mind it a bit.

"Sergio across the street will send his daughter to make dinner every night. I know you'll get by for lunch. And I'll call at least twice a week. Just so you know."

Just so he knew.

Just so he knew that she was alive, still breathing, still gasping in great big breaths of beautiful, fragrant air. His lovely girl.

"Where are you planning to go, sweetheart?" he asked her. Wherever it was, he wouldn't follow. The desert was his home, the wild animals prowling around inside his skin. The sun had baked itself right into his psyche, and if he walked too far past its borders, he would collapse into sand that filled his shoes. He knew that Bryony would come home, one way or another. She would either visit or be shipped home in bits and parts. The desert would have her when all was said and done, but not yet. Not quite yet.

"I'm not sure yet, Daddy. I was thinking that maybe I'd like to see cornfields."

"All of the old horror movies revolve around cornfields."

"Or New York City."

"You'll be murdered in no time, that be true."

"How about . . . the Northwest?"

"Ah, honey, serial killers spawn there. I don't think you'd last a day, dear heart."

Bryony shook her head. Her hair fell in golden waves down to her waist, pulled back by a headband, the way that a good girl wears her hair. Red Riding hood wore headbands, as did Alice in Wonderland.

Both were in peril. Both suffered. This fact was not lost on her father.

"Daddy, I want to see things. I want to be somewhere that I have never been before. I hate the desert, and want to be somewhere different."

Stop pulled himself up from the lawn chair. He hugged his girl.

"Don't be letting me stop you, Bryony. You go and be what you need to be. Do what you need to do. You know that I'll always be here, yes? Go be free, sweetheart. Live a good life."

Bryony skipped inside, much lighter after this conversation with her father. Stop sat himself back down on the chair in the tender way that he had picked up over the last eighteen years. She was a good girl, a sweet soul. Somehow she took whatever was in her hands and threw it across the sky like diamonds. This was what she needed to do, and the world needed her as much as she needed to see what life was like outside of a town built on death.

But he was sure going to miss her.

Stop stayed up very late that night, staring out at the desert. He learned long ago not to turn on the lights, to let the darkness creep closer. He didn't want to know what was staring back. Staring at him, and staring at his little girl.

Chapter Five
A Killing Sort of Love

Bryony ran.

She ran for many years, bouncing in and out of school, and discovering that she did not care for (in this order): journalism, engineering, dancing, creative writing, psychology, or dirt biking. Dirt biking was more of a fluke, a class that she joined in an out-of-this-world moment of sheer whimsy, because she wanted to do something fun and free and different. The bike itself wasn't a problem, but a bike plus dirt equaled a hot, cranky, sweaty Bryony, and that is never a good thing. So, no. Dirt biking was right out.

But a degree is a degree, regardless of what it is in, and all of the world looks fondly upon said degree, so Bryony slogged through her psychology classes. She also briefly considered Criminology, but figured that most of the people there weren't as interested in capturing criminals as they were about criminals learning to avoid being caught. She was a butterfly, fluttering around joyfully. She was not stupid.

But she was also curious about love. She wanted a real, true love that accepted what she was and how she was going to leave this earth, and didn't run screaming into the night from the crushing madness of it.

She tried on one young man after another, and it was a fun and happy time for all.

Oh, she tried on Brandons and Jordans and Nathans and Jeffs. She tried on a Raoul and a Rhett and even a Perry, but neither one of these fine gentlemen was exactly right for our diligent Bryony.

"I'm sorry," she said to each one, patting their cheek. "You are not for me, and I am not for you. Let us move on and be happy, yes?" And yes, each young man wanted to be happy, and each young man let her go, and some were actually quite relieved to shrug the burden of responsibility off their shoulders. Bryony was joyful and she was kind, but it couldn't be forgotten that death was constantly ruffling its fingers through her hair, and this was a difficult thing to accept. Still, one of the Brandons clung for a bit, which is to be expected every now and then, but when this particular Brandon met an especially dewy-eyed Matilda, everything set itself to rights.

Her first real boyfriend should have been a warning to her, but he had charm and, more importantly, he didn't immediately cut his eyes to Bryony when a girl from her dorm went missing, or when a young man from her study group was discovered hanging from the shower head.

His conversations started with, "How are you doing, love?" but after a while they changed to, "Are you all right?" and "Did anything dangerous happen today?" and "I had the most horrifying dream about you last night. You don't happen to be severed at the waist, do you?" When they embraced, he'd squeeze her so tightly she couldn't breathe, and then he'd run his hands down her shoulders and arms, checking for bruises and gaping knife wounds.

"Your neck is so very fragile," he murmured one evening, and Bryony had enough.

Really, she ought to have learned her lesson there, but love is ever so shiny and desirable, and so desperately worth pursuing, we are told, and so two Kens, a Nick, and a Johnny later she came across Jeremy, who was tall and darling.

"You're going to die, Star Girl," he said. His thick lashes dropped over his eyes.

"Yes, I know."

"That's cool."

They went on dates and to dances where he spun her until they both laughed. He hung his arm around her shoulders like he was hanging up a coat, and Bryony wondered deep in her heart if this was it, if this was truly how love was supposed to feel. Enchanting and giggly but somehow darkly lonely, as if Jeremy's breath stole a tiny bit of her soul each time they kissed.

One day she walked into her dorm room and found him sitting on her bed, holding a gun.

"I can't stand it anymore," he said before she even had a chance to open her mouth. "I can't stand the waiting."

Bryony stood still, her arms full of flowers gathered from the gardens outside. The breeze from the open window moved her hair and made the flowers dance gently.

"Run," the lilacs seemed to tell her. "Have you forgotten how? Have you forgotten what you do? Run, my girl, run!"

"I fantasize about killing you," he whispered. "I have done it a thousand ways. Poisoned you. Torn you apart with my bare hands. Snapped your bones and heard you sigh as your life ends."

"Run!" shrieked the lilacs again, and one threw itself from the bouquet and onto the floor.

"I think about it because I love you," Jeremy said. The gun twitched in his hand and Bryony saw his eyes were wild with rage and torment and, yes indeed, a killing sort of love. This nearly made Bryony smile.

"I mean," he said, standing and pointing the gun to Bryony's cheek, "if you are going to be murdered, shouldn't it be by me? Wouldn't that be kindness? Is it possible to love somebody any more than that?"

"You're stronger than this," she said, but even as she said it, she knew it wasn't true. It was a lie, oh, it was a lie, but she didn't know what else to say. "Please" or "Jeremy" or "I could maybe love you if you gave me more time", perhaps, but no, she said none of these things. She only said, "You're stronger than this."

"No, I'm not," he said sadly, and his finger moved on the trigger.

Bryony closed her eyes.

Chapter Six
Piece You Together

Bryony walked out of school with a degree and several quirky friends who despised each other greatly. But she often found herself thinking about how the smell of fireworks would forever remind her of gunfire and blood and of her dear Jeremy who, even with his skull in pieces, remained tall and darling. His death decorated her spirit with sharp, crystalline stars of sorrow, and this moved the hearts of her dear friends, who loved Bryony and vowed to come to her funeral when the time came.

"Poor girl, she is not long for this world," they all thought. "I wonder how they will do her hair when she is dead. I hope that they fill her casket with roses/irises/daffodils. I will write her a tragically romantic love note and slip it inside. I will shake the hand of her father. I will cry bitter tears and mourn her."

Then they all scurried back to work on their dissertations and fell asleep at their desks, dreaming sweet dreams of an exquisite corpse.

Bryony had dreams of her own. She took her

degree and promptly rejoiced. "Yay, yay, and hooray!" she said, and called her father, who did a little dance right there, holding the phone in one hand and his sagging trousers in the other.

"We're educated! We're educated!" he yelled, and they laughed and she bubbled and he bubbled back, and both were equal parts excited and relieved. When the talk finally died down some, Stop asked Bryony about something that he had been thinking upon for quite some time.

"So," he said calmly, like it ain't no thing, "what are your plans now, my girl?"

Bryony thought for a minute, and then she said, "Daddy, I think that I would like to fall in love."

Stop had often thought of this himself, and he nodded, although of course she couldn't see him. Stop was all for his little girl falling in love, because she had a lot of love to give. Hopefully she would meet a nice young man who had love to give back, and plenty of it, and it would be a happy and desirable affair. Still, being a father, and more importantly *her* father, he felt that he must do the responsible thing, which was to ask, "And what about your fate, Bryony? What will this boy do when he comes home one day, and he calls your name, but you are nowhere to be found? Or you are to be found, but scattered all over the room? Will he drop to his knees, kiss your hands and say, 'Oh, my darling, what have they done to you?' Will he then walk across the hall and collect your toes, and your arms, and sob into your bosom and legs, and piece you all together so that he can hold you one last time? Have you thought of this?" He knew that she had.

Her reply was instant. "Yes, Daddy. But the man

that I fall in love with will be strong enough to survive when I no longer will. He will be prepared. And he will love me all the more because he will understand what a fragile thing life is, and that every moment might be our last. And whenever we fight, he will call me up immediately and say, 'I'm so sorry, love, because I don't want those hateful things to be the last words that you ever hear from me. I love you, I love you, I love you.' Don't you think this will be the case?"

Stop knew this would be the case, because he felt that very same way about his daughter. It does teach you what real love is, knowing that it will be yanked away some day without your consent. It does make you appreciate that which will no longer be there.

"He will be a lucky man," he said, and he knew that Bryony was smiling on her end of the phone. "I wish you both well."

"Thanks, Daddy," she said, and promptly set about to fall in love. She read a book about orcas and fog and funny little sharks spotted in the Puget Sound, so she decided on a trip that would take her to Seattle. After moving, she followed a suggestion to wander Pike Place Market in the mornings, and her very first day there she saw a young man with too-long hair strumming his guitar with his case open at his feet. His name was Eddie, and he was constantly filled with sorrow, and he was beautiful, and she immediately knew that he was the man that she always wanted. She was ready for him.

Eddie, on the other hand, was not quite so ready for her.

Chapter Seven
Eddie Meets Bryony

*E*ddie Warshouski didn't have anything that he really loved besides his guitar. He called her Jasmine, and grudgingly shelled out the money so that he could buy the permit necessary to play her down at Seattle's Pike Place Market. The crowd was good there; happy, wide-eyed tourists, wide-eyed locals who came for the flowers and to support each other. They stopped by the first Starbucks and ogled the mermaid. They stopped by the tables and sampled honey and candies and pointed at the jewelry and crocheted hats that were always beautiful, but seldom sold. They made a solid wall of noise behind Eddie's brain, and he liked that. Anything to shut out the visions. Anything to shut out the voices.

Eddie put his head down and played.

His music got him through the days, and it was even more essential during the nights. He closed his eyes and picked out an intricate melody. He heard some change drop into his guitar case, and forced his lips into a congenial smile. Thanks, guys.

He peeked through his lashes at the slim girl who

was enamored with the display of flowers. Yellow daffodils, mostly, and something purple and feathery that he didn't recognize. She pulled a little coin purse from her pocket and reached deep inside. The smiling man working the flower station handed her a large bouquet, and the girl's hair fell in front of her face as she inhaled deeply. He had noticed her almost as soon as she arrived at the market, standing and staring open-mouthed at everybody rushing around her. She was a spot of color with her bright red coat and hat, white gloves and a scarf wrapped tightly around her throat. It wasn't that cold, so she wasn't from around here, not used to the weather. Her hair was curling in the sea air, looking like a frightened thing, and for some reason it almost made him smile. Almost, but not quite.

Chad, one of the fish throwers at the market, lasered his gaze at her. He was notorious for such things, and it didn't surprise any of the regulars when suddenly a fish came sailing her way.

She was unprepared, this ephemeral girl, and Eddie could tell by the way that she uselessly put up her hands that she wouldn't know how to catch a fish even at the best of times. It hit her square in the chest, knocking her flowers everywhere, and surprise more than force knocked her back. She fell onto the ground and began to cry.

Eddie wanted to help her almost as much as he didn't want to, but his fingers kept working on his guitar. He sent hateful vibes Chad's way, which was pretty much the worst that he could do at this point. A woman in a sari with blue hair helped the crying girl up while others scrambled around for her flowers. She was on her feet by the time that Chad had wound his way through the crowd.

"I'm so sorry," he said, sounding truly sincere, which was part of his gift. Oh, if only Chad used it for good! "I didn't mean to frighten you, and I especially didn't mean to knock you down. It's only a stuffed fish that we throw for fun sometimes, to surprise the crowd. Are you all right?"

He took her by both hands, and smiled down at her with what he assumed was a charming air. The women in the crowd leaned into it, a compass pointing to True North. Eddie turned his face away.

"I'm fine," the girl said, and everybody sighed in relief. She was fine. The poor, tragic thing had been shaken, true, but now she had her wits about her. Several hands dusted her off and patted her hair caringly, pressing her bouquet back into her hands. This man will take care of you, the hands said. He's a good-looking man, a nice man, a man who will sweep you off your feet and carry you to places of wondrous delight. Stick with this man, this fish-thrower named Chad. He's the one for you!

Eddie's snort was inaudible beneath the hum of the crowd. He didn't look as Chad apologized and offered to make it up by taking her out to dinner. He let his eyes roam up to the white clouds in the sky. It was a clear day, a rare day. Beautiful, really, if he cared about such things. Which he didn't.

He heard her voice, soft and sweet. "No, that really isn't necessary, thanks. I don't go out with people I don't know. It's very dangerous. Perhaps we could become friends first."

Eddie's eyebrows shot up, and this time he couldn't help it; he smiled.

Chad's voice was smooth. "Don't you go out with people? To get to know them?" Eddie was certain that he was grinning charismatically. The girl would have no chance but to fall.

"No, I don't."

"Not ever?"

"Not ever."

Eddie played something wryly morose on his guitar. It accentuated the situation perfectly, and the man next to him laughed. Eddie went back to his earlier melody again, refusing to acknowledge that he was listening. They were all listening, and they knew it, and everybody knew that they knew it, but still they pretended otherwise. The crowd was instantly absorbed in rifling through their purses, fluffing out their hair, making sure that all packages and large bouquets of flowers were wrapped and carried properly. They were all here by happenstance, and it wasn't anybody's fault that they were obligated to overhear this rather embarrassing conversation taking place in plain view. The crowd pressed closer.

Chad's smile was starting to falter, lips closing around his white teeth until they barely peeked through. This was not turning out as planned. The girl with the starry eyes obviously sensed his discomfort, because she clasped his fishy hands with her pristine gloves.

"Oh, I do hope that we can become dear, dear friends!" she said sincerely, and stood on her tiptoes to kiss him on the cheek. Chad blinked and the smile came back to his face. Eddie's guitar made an uncharacteristic TWANG! that quickly became something quirky and full of snarky delight. Nice save, Eddie.

Chad was called back to work by his manager, who grew tired of his employee's frolicking. Chad shot the girl a genuine grin and bounded off.

Eddie kicked the melody up a notch, and it became a fine, jaunty song. The girl's head turned until her eyes rested on his guitar, and slowly they traveled up until they met his.

She smiled at him, and tossed a flower into Jasmine's guitar case, but her good humor dropped away when she saw the expression he wore.

The girl automatically reached out for him, but he jerked away from her, and she recoiled.

Her eyes said that never in all of her life had anybody treated her like that. Never had anybody glared at her with all of the horror and hatred that this young man did.

A stranger from the crowd put his hand on her shoulder and a young woman impetuously threw both of her arms around the Star Girl, who looked stricken, stricken, as she watched the young guitar player sling his instrument over his back and run

run

run

run away.

Chapter Eight
The Significance of Words

The reason for Eddie's abrupt and discourteous departure is this: When he met Bryony's eyes, he was nearly knocked down by the force of her soul. A sweet soul, to be sure, but a strong soul. A courageous and carefully optimistic soul, and a soul that would be forced to endure the most gruesome and unspeakable tragedy. She would be broken, and razored, and her pink lips and her soft fingers and the insides of her elbows, and oh, oh, oh! Her fate was carefully engraved onto the irises of her eyes with jewelers' tools, and Eddie couldn't deny what he saw. She seemed like such a nice girl, a delicate thing that had fallen down from the stars, and the horrors that would befall her were . . . they were too much. Eddie couldn't do it again.

Wait, what was that? Eddie couldn't do it *again*, you wonder?

Such a difference one little word makes. Such weight and significance that word carries. If Eddie couldn't do it, well, then, certainly it could be understood. Who wants to see a lovely young girl fall to the scythe? But if Eddie couldn't do it *again* . . .

My, my. Certainly that does change everything, doesn't it?

Chapter Nine
Disconsolation

Chad the Fish Guy almost regretted knocking the mysterious girl down and making her cry, except that he never really regretted anything. Chad did what he did and then it was done, and what a simple and unimposing world this was for him. This meant that he ate whatever he wanted to eat with no regard for his health, and yelled at whoever he wanted to yell at out on the street, which happened more times than even he would perhaps care to admit. When he found a particularly pretty girl (which happened more nights than not) he smiled his charming smile and took her out to dinner and then brought her home and then kicked her out. He never saw her again, and if her feelings were hurt and she cried into her teddy bears or whatnot, well, that didn't really concern Chad now, did it?

"Well, perhaps it concerned him, maybe a little bit," you say, because you are a sweet and gentle reader, and are apparently hoping for the best. And that is very gallant of you to think, but no, you'd be wrong. For Chad thought of nobody but himself. And why is this, one might wonder? Is it because he wasn't loved enough as a child? Is it because he was born with blackness where his heart should be?

This naturally segues into the concept of killers and evil and those who prey on sweet little things.

At this your ears will prick, and you will immediately seize upon the idea that Chad is the killer, the one who will end Bryony's life. You will shout: "No, don't go in there!" whenever she enters into a room with him, and you will flinch whenever he hands her a flower or a particularly fine piece of fish from his stand at the market, and you will die a little inside if or when he leans down to kiss her one excellent evening under the moon, if things don't chance to work out with Eddie.

It is very easy to jump to conclusions, is it not? Yet if one does this thing, life will constantly disappoint. One does not know the heart of Chad the Fish Guy, and what his true intentions are deep inside.

Perhaps the one who is the least in touch with Chad's heart is the infamous Chad himself. Did he spend too much time alone as a young boy? Are his parents somehow to blame?

Of course not. Sometimes these things happen, and there is little or nothing that can be done about it. Chad the Fish Guy grew up to be a handsome, selfish man, and that is simply the way of it.

Chad was walking through the local Safeway, peering at the colorful packages on the shelves. He threw a couple of frozen dinners into his cart, and a few cans of soup. Tonight was to be a rare lone night for him, one where perhaps he could spend the time peering deep into his soul and ponder the future of his life and whether it was heading where he wanted it to go. Wouldn't that be a fine thing!

Alas, it is not how Chad will choose to spend his evening.

He will eat his frozen meal that he will only cook partially because his microwave is on the fritz, and he will watch an old movie with some rather crude and derogatory humor that will leave him strangely hollow inside. He will take a shower and dry himself off with a garishly patterned towel that he will then throw on the floor. He will crawl into his bed and he will curl up on his side and fall asleep alone. He will have a rather odd dream about mechanical porpoises and white trains speeding through tunnels with robots cavorting about on top. He will wake and think about the pretty, ethereal girl at the market, and again puzzle about why she rejected him, but shrug his shoulders and decide that a soon-to-be-dead girl sounds like trouble, anyway.

Let us hurry ahead to the morning.

Chad checked out, and loaded his groceries into the trunk of his car, keeping a Mountain Dew to drink immediately. He chugged it in under four seconds (almost breaking his own soda-chugging record; way to go Chad!) and then tossed the empty can into the dumpster behind the Safeway. It didn't land with a thunk or a clink or any of the delightful onomatopoeic sounds that an aluminum can makes when it hits the metallic floor of an empty dumpster. Therefore the dumpster was at least somewhat full.

"Why on earth would we care?" you ask in exasperated confusion. "Does it matter to me if the garbage men haven't emptied the dumpster beside a

Seattle Safeway? And what does this have to do with Chad the Fish Guy? Why am I following him only to find out that he's throwing cans in dumpsters? Why, that's hardly sinister at all!"

Ah, truly brilliant reader. You are so accurate, and yet so misled at the same time.

The drinking of the soda is not nefarious, nor is the tossing of it into the dumpster. Rather, this is a good thing to learn about our Chad, for now we know that he chooses not to litter, and if life is about keeping score, then this is a point in his favor.

But the fact that the dumpster is not empty, well, that turns out to be a very poor thing indeed, at least, for somebody.

No, more than that.

It turns out to be disconsolation for several somebodies.

Chapter Ten
Of Murder and Flowers

The very day that: 1) Chad threw a stuffed fish at her, and 2) Eddie ran away, Bryony landed a delightful little job assembling bouquets of flowers at the market.

"Excuse me," said a small round-faced girl with beautiful, dark almond eyes, "you seem very nice, and you also seem lost. May I help you somehow?"

Bryony was quite taken with this child. "Why, yes. I am looking for a job. Do you know anybody who is hiring?"

Suddenly every shop and station and table had a desperate need for more employees, sometimes kicking present employees out in order to make more space. Who didn't want a tragically sorrowful girl who chose to wear a happy smile around? Human nature dictates that we want what we want, and we want what is scarce. We want to enjoy things before they are taken from us. And this girl was defying fate by standing there this very minute. She should be dead by now, she was already lost. They grasped onto her life like a string of pearls.

The little round-faced girl worked at a flower stand,

and they needed more help (really, truly, they actually did), and Bryony was named for a flower, and saw very few in the desert, so she was delighted to accept the position. The vendors around rehired their old employees ("Come on back, Joe, I was only kidding,") and things fell into a pleasant routine at the market.

Until the woman in the stall next to Bryony's was found one rainy afternoon, stuffed into a dumpster behind Safeway.

Her hands and feet were bound, and her thick black hair had been shaved. Her eyes were missing, and were never found, actually, although the police looked for several years. Beautiful young women need their eyes, that's just the way of it. But, alas, this was never to be. An empty Mountain Dew can lay atop the body, with DNA on it. The owner of this DNA was hauled in for questioning by a Detective Ian Bridger and was treated rather meanly, when it came right down to it, but eventually he was let go. A man drinking a soda and throwing it away in a dumpster is most likely not a criminal, although his name will be filed away in the department's files for the future, if it is necessary.

Chad the Fish Guy hoped with all his might that it would never be necessary, and vowed to be A Very Good Boy from then on, only participating in Good Boy activities. He only kept up this vow for a week or so, but even that is better than nothing.

Word spread through the market quickly.

When she heard, Bryony sat down hard.

"It's happening again," she said quietly. Somebody ran to fetch a paper cup full of water.

"What is happening?" asked Clifford, the old man

that worked next to her. His real name was exotic and hard to pronounce, and he didn't want anybody to really try. He was especially fond of *Cheers* when he first came to the states and chose to go by Clifford forever more.

Bryony turned to Clifford and took hold of his withered hands earnestly. He flushed slightly under his leathery skin, but the storm light of the day hid it nicely.

"Clifford, wherever I go, women get murdered. Little girls. The first crush that I ever had, a beautiful boy on his skateboard, and a man who loved me enough to murder himself instead. It's as if death is a bolt of lightning, and it's striking all around me, looking for its target."

"Death isn't a very good shot," said the round-faced girl, and everybody in the flower section nodded in agreement.

Bryony sighed. "I don't know what to do. This always happens. I keep moving and moving, but no matter where I end up—"

"Don't worry about it," Clifford said kindly, patting her hands. "We'll protect you. We're not scared of no curse—"

"It's not a curse," said Bryony.

"—of no magic spell—"

"I don't believe in magic," said Bryony.

"—of no strange *birthright*—"

Bryony didn't have anything to say to that one, and Clifford smiled and continued. "So don't be worried for us, and we'll take care of you. Nobody will have you, our sweet flower girl. Nobody."

It was a fine sentiment, and greatly appreciated,

even if everybody there knew it was completely untrue. Nobody could protect her, nobody could stop it. For a moment Clifford believed it himself . . . almost. Then his face faded as reality struck, and he was a bent, translucent man. His desire was pure and protective, though, and it made Bryony happy.

"Thank you, Clifford," she said, and there were smiles all around.

Death had not touched her. Not yet.

"But it will," said a voice, and they all turned to see Eddie leaning against a pillar. He scowled at them. "Don't be fooling yourselves."

He turned and stomped off, and the crowd reacted as if it were a miniature Running of the Bulls, diving and leaping out of his way to avoid the inevitable carnage that would ensue on contact.

"I don't understand him," Bryony said softly. "He seems to dislike me so much."

Eyes met, heads nodded in silent communication. The young girl with almond eyes put her arms around Bryony.

"I think he likes you just fine. Probably more than he would prefer. You see—"

"No, don't tell me," Bryony said. She stood up, gathered a handful of flowers. "I am going to ask him myself. Wish me luck."

Good luck and wishes and prayers abounded.

She pulled her red coat tighter around herself, held the flowers delicately, yet firmly under, her arm and started off after the tortured and unamicable Eddie.

Chapter Eleven
Broken Glass and Jonquils

"I *hate you*, Bryony," Eddie said.

It absolutely wasn't true, and Bryony wasn't there to hear it, but it was good practice.

Eddie stormed up the street away from Pike Place. He was looking for a bar, or a club, or somewhere he could duck out of sight and brood on exactly how much he desired to dislike Bryony. She with her wide eyes and sorrowful ambiance. He would find her one day in pieces, or not find her at all, and which would be worse? It was like the time—

"Eddie Warshouski, I brought you some flowers. Now why don't you like me?"

Bryony offered the flowers to him as if they were a sword. He had never felt so threatened by jonquils before. He took a step back, nearly falling off the curb, and this made him angry.

"Why are you following me?" he demanded.

"I told you, I brought you some beautiful flowers." Bryony shoved the flowers into his face. They smelled divine, or at least they would have if Eddie sniffed at them, but he didn't. He was too angry. He merely inhaled to *breathe*, and the scent of the blossoms invaded his nose, uninvited. It was a Trojan Horse scenario, where oxygen was necessary and good, and riding upon it was the conniving perfume of greenery and flowers, and who was he to keep it out? He needed to breathe, after all. Breathing sustained life. Eddie chose life. And if life comes with the divine decadence of jonquils, then so be it.

Bryony smiled. "You like them! They do smell wonderful, don't they?"

"I hate jonquils," said Eddie.

Bryony's smile grew wider, more radiant. Eddie shielded his eyes from it. "Ah, but you know what they are called, and that says a lot about you. Few people take the time to learn the names of flowers, and jonquils especially aren't well known. Everybody thinks that they are daffodils. You don't hate them at all, or else you wouldn't be so aware."

"So I picked up a few things from playing next to a flower shop. So what?" Eddie grabbed the flowers out of her hand, daring her. Daring her to what? He didn't quite know, but he was going to dare her all the same.

"I'm named after a flower," she told him. "A plant used for healing." Her spirit practically shimmered in front of his eyes and went out.

Just like Rita had, way back when. Only Rita hadn't been marked for death, she was just an innocent passerby, like those caught in fate's range of fire.

"Bryony can also kill you," he pointed out bitterly. She opened her mouth to say something when suddenly there was a popping sound and a store window shattered behind her.

Glass flew through the air like vapid ballerinas. For

a second, everything paused, and Eddie allowed himself to gaze at Bryony's pale face as she was stopped in motion, her hair swirling through the air like mist. Her eyes were large and they hid nothing, broadcasting her emotions like a satellite dish. He could plainly see her wonder at the world, and a kind of shocked amazement that something was exploding behind her so unexpectedly, and a little bit of . . . Could that be true? Is there some anger there? Why, yes! There is anger! A type of smoldering fury that made Eddie's lips twitch a bit, until he realized she was probably angry at him for making such a spectacle of himself, for being so harsh toward her all the time. And he had been cruel; he admitted it, distancing himself from this woman who dragged the mantle of certain destruction behind her like a ragged blanket. She wore it so well, with such grace, that he half supposed that she wrapped herself rather primly in it at night, that it was her choice. Never did it occur to him that perhaps this wasn't something that she chose to bear, that she ran long and hard from it day after day, only giving in graciously after her brief break for freedom. Nobody really wants to be murdered.

After Rita's bloody demise, which was traced to the man who lived two floors under her, Eddie ceased to live. The enormous change it wreaked on his life, the visions he saw behind his eyes when he went to sleep, the sly glances the police gave him as they ceaselessly questioned him down at the station, until the real murderer found, of course . . . This haunted a man. He couldn't, he wouldn't, do it again. Ever. End of story.

He nodded curtly at Bryony, who was still in suspended animation, glass diamonding her hair, frozen in the process of hitting the ground. Hitting the streets of Seattle, why? Oh, yes, because there was a bullet. A bullet ripping the air asunder as it looked for a place to land that wasn't glass, wasn't brick and stone, but was something warm, something that would give underneath its nose, something that would invite it in to ricochet around until it found soft veins to decimate and organs to puncture.

Until it found Bryony.

Suddenly the world sped up again, the background music of life lurched up to its normal, frenetic tempo. Bryony fell to her knees, covering her head with her arms and curled up into a ball on the sidewalk. Eddie huddled beside her, and there was more noise or maybe it was screaming coming from one or the other or both of them, he could never be certain.

A man was on the ground, not far from them, his cap knocked off and his hair running red. Shopping bags lay beside him, and Eddie noticed detachedly that he had been shopping at Nordstrom Rack, at Sharper Image, at Old Navy. A pair of small tennis shoes peeped out of one bag, tiny little things, shoes that would appear on the feet of a child just learning to walk. Strangers had gunned down somebody's daddy.

Eddie realized Bryony was shaking the glass out of her hair frantically, while she rocked back and forth.

"Why? Why?" she screamed, and Eddie was shocked to see her in such a panic, surprised at how her earlier serenity and weary acceptance of her fate had crumbled away. He reached out a calloused hand to her, but stopped just short of stroking her hair, because he didn't want to commit, didn't want to touch her because then he would be drawn into her world, and he knew it. He knew it was a dark world of twisted mirrors.. It was a torturous place where she would forever be denied any semblance of rest, and would have to be vigilant. One night she would be too exhausted to lock every door and check every window. On that night, a neighborhood monster would sneak in and flay all that was living from her.

Even now the monster's breath fogged her window. Even now it watched.

Eddie's hand hovered half an inch away.

Bryony's face was streaked with tears. "Why do they all have to die? Why can't I just die, instead of seeing it miss me and take them over and over and over and over?" She looked at the dead father and sobbed, buried her face in her hands again. "I wish it was over, I wish that I was dead. But I want to live, I want to live!"

Our good and brave Eddie.

He knew the consequences he faced. He was intimately familiar with the awfulness of murder and the way it destroys everything from the inside out. There is the murder itself, a gruesome thing, and then there is the parasite it leaves behind, worming and gnawing its way through everybody near enough to touch. The paranoia of the landlord, the suspicion of the neighbors, the heartbreak of the church congregation and the guilt of the loved ones.

Oh, the guilt of the loved ones.

If I was better or stronger or smarter, Bryony, he thought, *I would be of more use to you.* He looked at the girl, who seemed smaller somehow, a crying doll. Tiny gems of window glass clung inside the curve at the top of her ear, and somehow that made his decision for him. It was such a vulnerable area, how could the glass even dare to fall there? He was incensed. He was outraged.

It needs be said that Eddie Warshouski didn't make the decision lightly, but when he did, he knew that he would never unmake it.

He grabbed Bryony, pulling her face into his jacket, whispering calming things in her ear, as they knelt together in a sea of sirens and blood and broken glass and scattered yellow jonquils.

Chapter Twelve
A Splendid Way to Go

"Daddy? Are you there?"

"My sweet girl! How is everything going?"

"Daddy, I met him. I met him, and his name is Eddie."

"Congratulations! And he's strong enough to handle you?"

"I think he is, although he doesn't know it yet. He'll learn, though."

"Are you going to bring him by sometime?"

"I will, Daddy. I want you to meet him."

"The desert has been howling for you at night, my dear. It's pacing back and forth in front of the house, leaving footprints in the sand. You need to be very careful."

"I will. And Daddy? He's going to love me. He's going to love me until both of our hearts burst from it all. Wouldn't that be wonderful? Wouldn't that be an absolutely splendid way to go?"

Chapter Thirteen
A Dangerous Path

Now you might think that Bryony lives alone because there was never mention of a roommate. It would be a wise thing, true. If those close to her tend to end up as casualties of the cosmos, it would stand to reason that she would choose not to inflict her delightful presence upon anybody else. However, this is Seattle, and as we all know, space is a precious commodity in any big city. Prices are high, and Bryony works arranging flowers at the market, not as the CEO of some prestigious and eyebrow raising company. Not that this is a path that she couldn't take, because she certainly could if she had the time and the inclination for it, but quite simply, the desire isn't there. She is happy to be a flower girl and spend her days watching cheerful people (and a few irritated ones) prancing through the market. She likes listening to Eddie as he plays his clever songs, and even sings once in a while. Above all, Bryony likes to be free. She always needs the choice of running to be available to her, as it has proved itself to be indispensable in the past. So a CEO she is not.

But a roommate!

Ah, yes, she has one, a pretty dark-haired girl with black eyes that dissect you into your molecular state as soon as she sees you. Her name is Syrina, and she is a theater student at the university, and also very poor, which is the topic of many a comfortable conversation in the evenings. Syrina cut Bryony's hair into something more adult, Bryony showed Syrina how to balance a checkbook, and they both spent many a night painting the inside of their closets bright, sunshiny colors together. Bryony feared greatly for her new friend's safety at first, but when Syrina's boyfriend Rikki-Tikki started spending more time at the apartment than out of it, Bryony felt much better. He was a large man with a Don't-Murder-My-Girlfriend type of nature, and this was comforting. Naturally his Xbox controllers ended up in strange places like in the refrigerator and in Bryony's closet, but if a small inconvenience now and then meant one less murder in the apartment, it was most certainly worth it.

"Syrina," Bryony said this particular evening, "I think that there is something missing in my life."

"What's that?" asked her roommate, making something exotic and delicious for dinner, as she was wont known to do.

"I'm not exactly sure. Perhaps there is something that I want to do, only I'm not, and I don't know what it is."

Syrina sat down and slid a plate of mysterious deliciousness over to Bryony. "I know what you should be doing, Star Girl. You need to run."

"You want me to leave?" Bryony asked, and her face fell. She was dearly enjoying this town, and these people, and this apartment, and her roommate, and this food. It was spicy and made her nose run slightly. It also made her eyes tear, or maybe that was simply the sting of Syrina's suggestion.

"No, you silly girl," Syrina said, and swatted at her roommate playfully. "When I said 'run,' I meant 'run.' Like I do. To keep in shape, so I can fit in my costumes. To quiet my mind. And you, my friend, really need to quiet your mind."

Bryony was intrigued. All her life she had been running, but now she could physically? Honestly? Truly? Run away?

"What do I need to get started?" she asked.

Syrina spoke through a mouthful of food, which was improper, of course, but certainly excusable because she was home and with a close friend, and was famished.

"You'll need some shoes. That's pretty much it. Find a fabulous place to run. In fact, I suggest that you go to the Burke-Gilman Trail."

"Ooh, that sounds lovely! I'll start tomorrow, then! The Burke-Gilman. Thank you, Syrina. You really are such a good friend to me."

She was, too. A loud girl, a sometimes impolite girl, but a kind girl all the same. She truly thought she was doing Bryony a favor. Running, if one takes to it, is a wonderful thing, a time to calm your emotions and work your mind and your body. She was certain that Bryony would, indeed, take to it, since she was adept at running. She had, as she had immediately seized upon, been running her entire life. Only now . . . perhaps she'd be getting some real use out of it.

What Syrina didn't factor in was what she tried to

ignore. She tried harder than anybody else ever had, and at times was fairly successful. Her theater training helped her do this, she liked to think, and hoped it proved how fine an actress she was. She attempted to turn a blind eye to Bryony and the death that awaited her. She defied it, really, and that is why she suggested jogging on the Burke-Gilman; to flaunt Bryony's life and vitality out in the open where it could not be missed. She hoped staring fate right in the eyes would somehow make it shrink away and throw its hands in the air, saying, "All right, all right, you can have the girl. I don't need her, truly."

So run the Burke-Gilman trail, Bryony. Run fast and run well, and see if fate can catch you.

Because lately, you see, more and more girls have gone missing there. But surely that won't happen to her, of course not. After all, she has lived this long, hasn't she?

She has. Which means her time is coming closer and closer and closer. Fate can't be thwarted forever. But Syrina, who certainly means well, wasn't thinking of it this way.

Which was a rather large mistake indeed.

Chapter Fourteen
Her Fragile Hand

Eddie woke up one morning and realized that he had fallen for Star Girl. He knew that it would come to pass, and although grudgingly displeased with it at first, he soon came to accept the idea. He watched her as she laughed with her friends at the market. He watched as she talked wildly with her hands, explaining something to Chad the Fish Guy. He fantasized about beating up Chad the Fish Guy, out in the parking lot, preferably. When the sun was down and the cops were all looking the other way. What he would really like to do would be to tie him up and throw him off the pier and into the sea, but Eddie realized that was going a little far. A man could dream, however.

Speaking of dreams: A man walked by, eating a fresh miniature doughnut from the vender, and stopped abruptly when he heard Eddie play.

"I like that song, boy. Did you write it?"

"Yes, sir," Eddie said politely. He could be extremely polite if he wanted to, and something about this man's tailored slacks and friendly face told him that he wanted to.

The man dug into his wallet for a five dollar bill and tossed it in Eddie's guitar case. He also tossed in a business card.

"Give that number a call," he said. "I'd be interested in having you play down at the station."

The station in question was a local radio station that had an eclectic play list, and apparently Eddie and Jasmine were off-kilter enough to fit right in. He could hardly wait to tell Bryony, although he was trying to keep it cool. Cool. He was going to keep it so extremely cool that—

"Hey, Bryony, guess what? I've been invited to play at the station, wow, just out of the blue and this could be my big break so what do you think of that?" he said in one breath. He was fairly glowing, a nuclear bomb of joy.

"Why, Eddie, that's wonderful!" she exclaimed, and threw herself in his arms, a flurry of hair and ribbons and fuzzy teddy bear excitement. Eddie glanced over to see if Chad the Fish Guy was watching, and he was, wringing a nice bit of salmon too tightly in his hands. Eddie allowed himself to smile.

Bryony pulled back. "So when are you going to go down?"

Eddie shrugged, and Jasmine the guitar, slung over his shoulder, shrugged, as well. "I'm not certain, yet. I need to call them and set something up."

Bryony smiled. "Well, I for one am exceptionally proud of you. You write the most beautiful music, Eddie." He blushed and she pressed forward. "You *do*. It's exquisite and intricate and fairly drips with burden. You write the most joyful songs of heart wrenching loss that I have ever heard. I love to listen to you in the background while I work."

"You think all of my songs are about loss?"

"Oh, aren't they? I can't hear the words over the crowd, just the melody. Am I wrong?"

No, she wasn't wrong. He just had never thought about it. He wrote songs about life, and if life includes loss, well then. Nobody ever mentioned it to him before. But then again, most people didn't mention much to Eddie Warshouski. Ever. His cutting glances and unpleasant scowls served to keep himself well isolated from mainstream society. Or even the outer fringes of society. From everybody, really, and that was just how he liked it, usually. Or at least, that was how it had been, before Bryony and her cursed glittering eyes.

Eddie's life *was* a life of loss. Almost everything that he loved had been taken from him at one time or another. He almost felt as though *he* were the one that fate toyed with, as if it was *his* fault Bryony suffered. If he was created only to have things taken, then wouldn't it make perfect sense that the young lady who would make him the happiest would be destined to fall in the most grisly manner imaginable? He felt he should apologize. He felt he should turn tail and run.

"Eddie," she said, and slipped her fragile hand into his. She had never done this before, and Eddie was instantly nervous. Would he hold it the right way? Did she want her thumb crossed over his, or his crossed over hers? Would he start to sweat, would it be unnatural, would the touch of his thick fingers send her into a tailspin of revulsion? What if they weren't shaped right, or he wasn't who she really wanted? Perhaps some other man with absolutely perfect hands was wandering the city, and she would try on hand after hand like Cinderella's slipper until she found the one who fit, and—

"Eddie, I like you very much, and I'm sorry for that."

Eddie, who was near to hyperventilating, looked at her sharply. "You what? And you're, huh?"

Bryony met his eyes briefly, and all of the ghosts and the demons, the horrors and the tremendous weight of her constant waiting rose up in a wave behind her, pressing down on him with so much force he felt he was sinking to the floor. It was too much, too much.

Bryony looked away, and Eddie's heart shivered again, one weak, shuddering spasm, and then it cheerfully fell back into its regular reggae rhythm.

"I know about Rita, and I am sorry," Bryony said. "I know how hard it is to be around me sometimes, for everybody, and I know it must be especially difficult for you. But I like you, you see, and I just want to be by you. I want to press my cheek against your jacket and see what your hair feels like. I love to listen to you play, and I pretend sometimes you wrote a song just for me. And all of this, it isn't fair to you, and for that I feel regret."

Regret. What an unusual choice of words. It isn't wise to regret, not really, and it usually doesn't do any good either. You regret things that happened and which you no longer have control over. You don't regret the present, and you don't regret the future. Bryony tended not to regret at all, it was just in her nature to accept all and carry on. But Eddie? She regrets being a bother to him? This made Eddie delightfully happy.

"Bryony, there's something that I have been wanting to give you—"

Ah, but fate intervenes as it always does, and suddenly Bryony's little flower station was overwhelmed with customers.

She was forced to return to work before Eddie had a chance to give her the shining gift that he had carried around in his pocket for the last three days. Even more importantly, she did not get the opportunity to tell him that she had begun running the trail, which she found difficult yet delightful, and a new running hunger had been born inside of her. If Eddie had known this, he would have immediately been concerned for her safety and demanded to run alongside her.

You see, the trail is where the murderer first spotted our Bryony.

Chapter Fifteen
I See You

The girl caught his eye immediately.

She was new to running, new to the trail, and her cheeks were rosy in the misty light. There was something about her, something special, a wobbling beacon shining up to the sky, only she wasn't calling down the stars.

She was calling him.

And being a man of great appetites he obsessed to satiate, he knew he would answer her. Because, you see, that is the way it works, and has always worked, and this man somehow knew the girl's whole life had been leading up to this moment.

Wonderful. Simply wonderful.

Chapter Sixteen
Live A Thousand Years

Rikki-Tikki and Syrina were watching a movie. They had reached that lazy part in their relationship where he was allowed to gain a few pounds and she was allowed to wear sweats, and occasionally go without makeup, and throw her hair back in a ponytail. All of this was perfectly acceptable and downright cozy.

Although the term used was 'watching a movie', it would be more accurate to say a movie was on and they weren't exactly watching it. They were dishing up bowls of ice cream and kissing in between strawberry spoonfuls, and Rikki-Tikki was telling Syrina about Samoa. He was also asking if she'd like come home with him sometime to meet his family, and Syrina was equally parts excited and nervous. What if they didn't like her? What if she didn't like Samoa? What if it all agreed with her so much that she never wanted to return home? How delightful! During this conversation, Rikki-Tikki brought up the subject of Bryony.

"Syrina, she is going to die, and I think you just don't want to accept it so much that you're not even paying attention to it. I know it's easier for you, but it isn't fair to the girl. She needs our support, to know we'll continue on after she's gone, that we'll remember her. She needs—"

"Rikki, why do we have to talk about this?" Syrina interrupted. She was getting exasperated and edgy, and talking about Bryony's fate really was quite out of the question and upsetting to her. Somebody so gentle shouldn't have to die, not ever, not even when they are ancient. It seemed like a cruel prank somebody had been playing on Bryony all her life, and Syrina just wasn't going to have it. It was her fiercely nurturing way, and she was ready to go the rounds with anybody who suggested Bryony might not be immortal, even if that person was her dearest Rikki-Tikki.

"I don't see any reason why she can't live a thousand years," Syrina said loyally, yet not altogether realistically. "She can live forever, if she really wants to. Who are we to say any different?"

Rikki-Tikki sighed, and put his arm around Syrina, who really was dealing with this entire situation the best way she knew how.

Syrina pretends, you see, and there is a safety in the pretending. The person she is onstage can get hurt and it doesn't affect Syrina. The words she says aren't hers; the ideas that are shot down belong to somebody else. If Syrina simply pretends hard enough, then it will all go away. Don't you see, Rikki-Tikki? It is her own way of protecting Bryony. It is her own way of surviving.

Rikki-Tikki is many things. He is kind and he is patient, and he is strong and steady like a great stone wall or a tree that you want to rest your back against when you are weary or in the midst of a fight. But most of all he is insightful, and listens to that little voice inside of his head and stomach that says "Stop pushing now," and "Perhaps you had better dig into this a little deeper" and even occasionally, "Your car keys are stuck between the cushions on the couch. Please be more careful with them in the future." And now this voice was warning him that Syrina's head was spinning with the thought that even her very finest effort at pretending might not be enough to keep her dear friend Bryony around. This is a harsh realization indeed, and one that Syrina particularly didn't want to face, so she chose instead to glower at Rikki-Tikki, who sighed and wisely kept the smile from his face.

"You're right, dear one," Rikki-Tikki said, and ruffled Syrina's hair. "We won't speak of such things. Not when there is such an entertaining movie on television."

In truth the movie was only subpar, and generally Syrina would pounce upon that sentence with a: "What, are you kidding? What horrid taste you have! Sometimes I wonder if we really have anything in common. The script is amateurish and the acting makes my brain want to burst out of my eyeballs!" But right now she was simply grateful for the distraction, as B-rated as it may be.

"Yes, you are absolutely right. Let us watch this movie about . . . radioactive giant grasshoppers. There really is nothing more in the world that I would rather do at the moment."

So he tightened his arm around her, and she rested her head upon his shoulder, and they both thought their separate thoughts.

Bryony will live forever, I know it, Syrina thought with a sternness that was endearing and also a bit frightening. *She will, she will. There simply can be no other way.* Then she vaguely wondered aloud if she should wear her purple high heels with her dress tomorrow or if she should just stick with fire engine red.

Rikki-Tikki's thoughts were like the sea, wide and deep and constantly shifting. He knew one day death would come for their dear friend, and there was no denying it. It did not do anybody any good. He also knew he wasn't ready for that time to be quite so soon, and he had a trick or two up his sleeve that could help stop it, at least for now.

"The purple," Syrina decided, and snuggled closer. Rikki-Tikki nodded his head, and Syrina took that as a positive sign toward her footwear choice. She had told him about all about dresses and shoes before. Use your hips to distribute the weight while walking, for example. Five-inch heels are sexy, but six-inches have just thrown you straight to trashy. Perhaps if Rikki-Tikki had been wholeheartedly engrossed in the conversation, he would have said yes, wear the purple, they all lovely and will convey everything you silently want to say about yourself. But what Rikki-Tikki was really nodding about was his decision: although it wasn't in his power to save Bryony, he was determined to try.

"It's getting late. Bryony should really be home by now," Syrina said. She kissed Rikki-Tikki and took their empty ice cream bowls to the kitchen. She stood at the sink and thought yes, Rikki-Tikki was right about Bryony's malevolent fate, but she couldn't let her mind explore the idea of a world without Bryony, because it would be a dim and cheerless world, an exceptionally ugly world, and nobody should be forced to live in such a lackluster place. Syrina was wiping a tear from her eye with the back of a soapy hand when she heard a strange sound from behind her. It was a furtive sound, a menacingly sneaky and surreptitious sound, a terrifyingly recognizable sound that announced, "Hello, I am everything you have ever feared and I have arrived."

It was the sound of a knife being quietly unsheathed.

Chapter Seventeen
A Delicate Guillotine

*B*ryony sobbed all of the way to the hospital, the note crumpled in her hand. Not Syrina. Not her dear, brave and true friend. It would be too cruel. It would be too much.

She ran through the hospital doors and up to the front desk.

"I am looking for my friend Syrina. Rikki-Tikki said she was here, and I'm so afraid! Is she alive? Is she hurt? Oh, won't you help me find her?"

The receptionist stared at this otherworldly woman whose soul was mixing with tears and spilling out of her ephemeral eyes. She wanted to grab the girl's mitten-covered hands and tell her stories about faeries and trolls and great green monsters born from gardens. She wanted to ask her if she thought it would hurt terribly when death came to take her, as it most certainly would. Why, perhaps even this very minute! Time is of the essence! The receptionist opened her mouth to speak.

"Bryony!"

Bryony spun around at the sound of Rikki-Tikki's voice and grabbed onto his sleeve.

"Is she dead? Did fate steal Syrina away? It was supposed to be me. It was supposed to be me!"

Rikki-Tikki smiled, and the tumultuous storm inside of Bryony's heart gave way to the clearing sky.

"She's all right. We've been in talking to a detective. Let's go see her, my girl."

He put his hand on the top of Bryony's head and steered her down the hall. Bryony chattered nervously the whole time, speaking with her hands and her voice and, most especially, her heart.

"Oh, you don't know how frightened I was. I saw your note saying that Syrina was in the hospital, and when I stepped into the kitchen and saw the blood on the walls . . ." Here her voice gave out, and Rikki-Tikki gave her hair a soft pat before leaning against an open door.

"She's here, Bryony. See?"

Bryony peeked inside the room. Syrina looked enraged and exhausted and very much alive.

Bryony threw her arms around her friend.

Syrina hugged her back. "You're okay! Thank goodness! I was so worried when you didn't come home on time, but now I'm so glad."

Bryony didn't realize she was crying again until Rikki-Tikki handed her a tissue. "I thought I had lost you. There was so much blood in the kitchen. Where did he hurt you?"

Syrina's eyes flashed. "Here. And here," she said, pointing out two small wounds in her hairline. "And he broke two of my nails. Not to mention here," she said, and revealed three long scratches on her wrist. "This is where he clawed me when he was trying to get away."

"When he was trying to . . . I don't understand. The blood!"

"It was the other guy's," Rikki-Tikki said. "I heard Syrina scream and I can't tell you how that felt, Bryony. Like I was sitting outside watching the moon and it just exploded in front of me. By the time I got there, she already had him backed into the corner."

"I threw some bowls at him," Syrina said. "I tried to find our kitchen knives but they must have been in the dishwasher, so I beat on him with a saucepan instead."

"You beat him pretty ruthlessly," Rikki-Tikki said. "I had to jump in to protect him. He seemed relieved to see me."

Bryony blinked at Syrina.

"But why?" she asked. "Why would you do something so dangerous? What if he had hurt you? Surely you understand the risk of just being my friend." Bryony stood tall, her fury hissed and mewed and wrapped itself brilliantly around her. "This is my burden to bear, not yours. I should never have asked this of you. I will go home and pack my things." She took Syrina's perfect dusky hands (save for the two broken and ragged fingernails) in her own. "I love you, and you are utterly exquisite and now you have been marred because of me. I have stayed too long."

Bryony kissed Syrina's cheek and turned to the door. It was blocked by Rikki-Tikki.

"Excuse me," she said to Rikki-Tikki. He just shook his head and crossed his arms over his chest.

"What a silly girl," Syrina said. She hopped off the table and stood beside Rikki-Tikki. She looked angry, amused, frustrated and frighteningly fierce. She was a radiant warrior, a delicate guillotine. Bryony very nearly wanted to step away from her, but then she remembered it was Syrina, and she felt brave again.

"I would die if you were hurt," she told Syrina. "I wouldn't want to live any longer."

"Bryony, don't you see the implication of what happened here tonight?"

Bryony didn't see. She saw that Syrina had walloped the daylights out of an unfortunate criminal who chose the wrong house to break into. She knew deep within herself that he had been wandering down a darkened street in the evening, and had said, "Gee, which home should I plunder this evening? I shall most certainly cause some wild mayhem." and she knew her apartment shone with a luminosity that made his heart pop with the brilliance of it, and he thought, "There, that's the place! Oh, the wonders I shall behold and the magnificent havoc I shall wreak." Only he didn't really partake in any scintillating misbehavior at all because Syrina swooped upon him with her fiery Saucepan of Vengeance, and Bryony felt quite sorry for our poor would-be murderer for a moment.

Syrina sighed. "The implication is this: that man came into our home in order to hurt you, but he failed."

"Because I wasn't home," Bryony said, and the tears almost started again. "I wasn't home and so you had to defend yourself against him."

Rikki-Tikki laughed. "She wasn't defending herself, Bryony. She was defending you."

"What?"

Syrina nodded eagerly. "Don't you see? He came in

to hurt you, and neither Rikki-Tikki nor I were going to allow it. That man slithered into our home with a weapon and I grew so angry. How dare he come after you. How dare he enter our home and try to draw the breath from your lips. Fate took a swing at you and what happened? We stood and we fought and we won. He'll go straight from the hospital to a jail cell, and we will never deal with him again. It is a wonderful thing." Why, Syrina looked quite drunk on her victory, and Rikki-Tikki smiled so hard that his eyes disappeared, and Bryony's heart began to lighten and turn its face to the sun and scream, "Yes! Yes, I have survived!"

"We won't leave you," Rikki-Tikki said simply, and for a brief second fate choked and quaked and drew back from the power of these two fierce protectors, who stood together in a united front between it and the Star Girl. How was it to get to her? It was much too difficult. After all of its work, plans, and delightful scheming. Everything was nearly lost.

And then fate shook its head and narrowed its eyes, growling deep in its throat as it remembered how crafty and venomous it could be. And when that venom is stoked by wrathful humiliation, well. Well. Careful, Star Girl. Your time has nearly come.

Chapter Eighteen
He Kills Again

*F*ate grumbled and schemed and plotted. Sending an enthusiastic but second rate robber to do a professional killer's job certainly didn't seem to work. Now the gloves were off. It was time to call in the big guns.

It is time to check in on our murderer.

What the murderer really wanted, of course, was Bryony. He did not know her name. He did not know anything about her. She could be a young doll-maker named Cassandra or she could be young man-turned-woman who was originally named Maurice, although he did not quite think so, and he had a fairly decent eye for that sort of thing.

But he also wanted to save her, as one saves dessert for a particularly fine reward for a job well done, a job like passing a grueling test at school or surviving this life, and thus he put Bryony away for later.

That did absolutely nothing to dispel the fact he wanted to kill now, and to make it good and satiating. One does not necessarily have to have crème brulee to satiate oneself. Certainly when there is no crème brulee to be had, one can do quite well with marshmallow rice squares made out of the cheap generic store brand cereal. There is no shame in this.

This particular victim was a girl that he saw shopping at a charmingly modest used bookstore that also doubled as a bakery, and she had exquisite calves. They reminded our killer of his days in junior high, where the girls had trim little calves that lengthened each time they had a growth spurt, and he would stretch his gangly legs out under their chairs so he could be as close to them as possible.

I shall call this girl Kathleen, he thought to himself (for Kathleen was the name of a girl that he had a shy fondness for when he was about fourteen). He followed discreetly as she hopped in her car and pulled off in the park to enjoy her scone and book. He hoped that this would be her destination, because he had it on good authority (his) that the women who exited this particular bakery/bookstore tended to be the type who headed outdoors to enjoy their lives, and they did things like knitting in the bright morning sunshine, or running around, laughing, with a red kite, and practicing tai-chi out in one of the many parks. This made him realize two things: 1) Bakery/Bookstores are good for the soul, and 2) they were also a fine place to prey.

"Excuse me," he said, stopping beside the woman as she read her book. She looked up, wiping bits of scone off from her lips.

"Yes?" she asked him with a barely detectable hint of nervousness.

"I'm sorry to bother you," he said, "but I happened to notice that you are reading the same book I am hoping to buy for my wife's birthday. Is it something that you would recommend?" A man walked by lazily, and the murderer's eyes followed him with studied nonchalance.

The woman, his "Kathleen," looked faintly surprised. "You want to buy your wife a copy of *Why It Is Prudent To Kill the Man That You Marry?*"

The killer's eyebrows raised a fraction before he could control them. "Why, uh . . . yes. Yes, I do. That is precisely the book that I wish to purchase. For my wife."

"Kathleen" shrugged, and the killer sighed in relief. The woman burst into a long and tedious book report using words like "feminist ideals" and "male oppressive dogs" and by the time they were completely alone and it was time for her to die, the murderer was very, very ready to kill her.

Chapter Nineteen
A Song

Eddie sat with his back against the cloying floral wallpaper in his apartment. He held Jasmine in his hands, and ran his fingers over her strings as he looked through the window. The moon was extravagant tonight. The stars were full of brilliant luster.

His fingers never ceased their movement and with his eyes full of the stars he teased out a song. It was something quite unlike anything else he had written before. It was about death and life and a plant that can heal or kill, respectively. It was a song about making the choice to love when you knew that in the end

. . . you would only have . . .

. . . empty hands.

Chapter Twenty
Be Aware

Syrina wasn't home when Rikki-Tikki came by, but that was all right. He mostly came to speak to Bryony.

"'Sup, girl," he said, and hugged her. She had spent the morning paying bills and making Very Important Phone Calls and decided to reward herself for the hard work. She was frosting cupcakes and was careful not to get the frosted knife in Rikki Tikki's dark hair when she hugged him back.

"Hello, how are things? Would you like a cupcake?"

He would like one, very much, and there was an impromptu cupcake party full of sprinkles and raspberry lemonade and good times and laughter. It was an enjoyable occasion, and funny stories were told, and each had the choice opportunity to see each other as the enchanting and mischievous beings that they had been as small children. But then it was time to get serious.

"They found another body, Bryony. A young woman with all of her limbs broken, stashed behind some trees in the park. She had some sort of book shoved down her throat, is what I'm hearing."

"Oh, how terrible."

"It's coming up on your turn, you know."

Well. He knew it, and she knew he knew it, but somehow the words still sounded unpleasant hanging in the air like that.

"Is it time for me to leave, Rikki?" she said. He was a big man, and a kind man, but most important of all, he was a wise man that listened to his gut and the wind. He watched things closely while the rest of them ran around in carefree bliss. Bryony trusted he would pick up on the subtle tell-tale signs the rest of them would miss.

He shook his head.

"Nah, it ain't time. Not to leave permanently, not yet, anyhow, but you need to be aware." He leaned forward. "I think it is time that you take Eddie home and pay a visit to your daddy. He needs to meet the man you're in love with, and the man that loves you."

Bryony smiled. "I don't know if Eddie knows he loves me yet. We haven't even gone out."

Rikki-Tikki rolled his eyes. "Girl, he knows. Doesn't sit well with him, but he knows." He looked at her meaningfully. "It's time for you to get out of here. Not for long, because I know fate can find you there, too, and quite possibly it is even more dangerous there. But, you'll have Eddie, and you'll have your daddy, and with the three of you standing arm in arm, I think you would have a mighty fine chance of surviving. Might even give fate a good ole kick in the eye, and I can't think of nothing better. But here? It's getting too hot around here right now. If you slow down for a second, I think you'll realize it."

Bryony patted his knee. "Thank you. You are a dear friend to me."

Rikki-Tikki grinned, and Bryony liked that. His teeth were white and happy and when he smiled, somehow the world seemed to be a better place.

"There's one more thing, kid," he said.

"What's that?"

"I think it's time that the ole Rickster teaches you how to box."

Chapter Twenty One
A Circle of Stars

Bryony didn't know why, but she was nervous the next time she saw Eddie. Usually she said what needed to be said without any embarrassment whatsoever, because honestly, who had the time to dance around what was really important? If there was something to be said, it should be said. There might not be a tomorrow, or even a later tonight. But something in her stomach flipped around, and when she saw Eddie at the market the next morning, she found herself suddenly not knowing what to say.

"I called the radio station," he said to her, and grinned. "I'm going down on Tuesday to introduce myself and play a couple of songs. Which ones do you think I should choose?"

She stared at him and her mouth worked, but nothing seemed to come out. Eddie's smile faded and he looked at her with some concern.

"Bryony? Are you all right?"

Suddenly she wasn't. She was tired, and scared, and the feeling of somebody's eyes on the back of her neck became more intense lately. Her daily boxing lessons with Rikki-Tikki made her feel strong and safer for the most part, but as she clenched her fists (careful to keep her thumb on the outside as he had demonstrated) it could not be denied that she was learning to defend herself from *someone*. Even if it was the palms of Rikki-Tikki's hands she was hitting, or an imagined foe she was kicking, there was a very real *someone* out there causing all of this commotion. If she was anywhere else, she would have run by now, picked up and moved to another destination, somewhere creative and new, where death wouldn't be able to find her. She would have blended in, she told herself, keeping her head low while people around her fell to the earth as their hearts stopped. Only she couldn't blend, had never been able to. Exquisite disaster perfumed her breath, and every eye always roved until they found her, and there it stuck.

But she didn't want to run. She wanted to stay here, with her friends, with her flowers, with Syrina who told her to start hitting the trails and suggested how to cut her hair, and Rikki-Tikki who was teaching her how to throw an effective right hook . . . and with Eddie. So much with Eddie.

There was no time. There was no time. There was no—

—time.

"I love you, Eddie Warshouski. I am going to die, very soon. I can feel it. It's coming closer and closer, and it's time for me to leave here, but I can't. Because I love you, and I think that you love me, too. I want you to come home with me and meet my father."

Well.

Well.

Eddie stuck his hands in his pockets. It looked like a defensive gesture, and something small, a bright and giggling thing inside of Bryony's heart clicked and broke, and she felt the pain of it as it rusted inside her chest. She had been so sure, and Rikki-Tikki had said it himself, and could it be true? Were they wrong? Could it be that perhaps Eddie didn't love her? The thought made Bryony slightly ill. Her head reeled.

"You're not looking so well, love," Eddie said, and helped her sit down.

"Yes, suddenly I'm not feeling so . . . what?" she said, staring at him with her large eyes. "What did you just call me?"

And Eddie did it. He couldn't help it, but the sight of her inquisitive gaze, with hurt dampening the edges, made the sharp metal cage around his heart give way.

Eddie laughed. He tipped his head back and he laughed long and hard. When he finally wiped his eyes and looked back at Bryony, she was disheveled and obviously more than a little bewildered.

"Are you . . . laughing at me?" she asked him in a tiny voice. Eddie pulled her from the chair and swung her around.

"No, not at all," he said. Then, "Well, yes. A little, but only in a good way."

"I . . . uh, okay," she said, and Eddie laughed again. He pulled something out of his pocket, which was the reason for putting his hand there in the first place.

"I've been trying to give this to you for ages, Bryony. And it just hasn't worked out. I didn't know how. But I saw this, and I thought of you, and I didn't know if giving it to you would mean anything, or if I would make a fool out of myself, or if you wouldn't like it or—"

"What is it?"

Eddie opened his hand, and inside laid a delicate bracelet made out of dozens of tiny silver stars. Bryony oohed.

"It's beautiful, Eddie. This made you think of me?"

"How could it not?" he asked, and carefully clasped the bracelet onto her wrist. Bryony held her arm to the light, and the stars twinkled and chimed.

"It really is one of the most perfect things that I have ever seen," she said, and the smile she gave Eddie made him know he had done the right thing, and for a second he was able to put the worries out of his mind. He knew as soon as he saw the bracelet was fashioned exclusively for Bryony, knew it would flow like water around the Star Girl's slender wrist while sitting stiffly and disappointedly on anybody else's. But he had hesitated. He had gone back to look at it in the case, again and again, pacing back and forth and trying to decide whether he should purchase it or not. Because he had visions, you see, pictures in his head of the way this would turn out. He would come home one day, either to visit her in her apartment, or perhaps (and this sent a little thrill through him) they would be married and he would return to the home they would share. "Bryony," he would call, taking his jacket off and draping it over a chair. "I'm home, darling." But there would be no answering call, no off-key singing in the back room while she dusted, and he would search the house for her, finding nothing, no trace. Until he came to the spare bedroom, where he would see something white and broken lying on the floor, barely peeping out from behind the bed. It would be her hand, he knew it, lying vulnerably with the palm up, the nails covered in blood and flesh that the police would later say wasn't hers. And for a second he would say to himself, no, that wasn't his Bryony, it was a discombobulated stranger that somehow ended up in the wrong house and had gotten herself killed. Yes, that is what happened except—

—except for the whimsical ring of stars circling her tender wrist and effectively destroying his desperate illusion, forcing him to see the bitter reality. Yes, this was his Bryony, and she had fallen, she had fallen, she hadn't been able to run fast enough or far enough this time.

Chapter Twenty Two
Dear Girl Who is Already Dead

This is what the murderer thought:

He thought, "The girl tends to come out in the early evening, except for Wednesdays. On Wednesdays she comes out in the morning when the mist still covers Matthews Beach. Useful."

He thought, "She always runs alone and then stretches out by the water. Useful."

He thought, "She tends to favor her right ankle, which seems to be a little unstable. Endearing, that. She is friendly to the other joggers on the trail, and doesn't mind falling into step with them temporarily, and will even chat with them. Useful."

He thought, "Something about her eyes. Something about the soft paleness of her throat. She seems to run above the ground, not necessarily across it. I think she was not created for this earth, but from the stars. And to the stars I will release her."

Briefly he thought that this could be a kindness, but then he pushed the thought away. He is not a man who dwells on being kind.

Her time is coming.

It is coming, but it is not quite here. He wants to watch her a little longer, the way that she often comes and swings on the swings after a particularly hard run, like she was a child. The way she climbs into the lifeguard's chair and gazes at the sky, or sits on the pilings and stares at the water.

Stares at the water.

Suddenly he thought of a gift that he could give her. It would be something very special, very personal for the Star Girl.

For the murderer had a hidden streak of romantic fancy inside of him, although he would slit your throat immediately if you so much as dared mention such a thing to him. But we are who we are, and deep inside the nearly impenetrable chambers of his heart, he wanted to do something small to make Bryony happy. He wanted to see her face alight with joy, to see her smile widen and know that he had caused it, to see the happy light burn bright in her eyes before snuffed it out permanently. This was what he thought about as he lay in bed at night.

"Dear girl who is already dead," he said out loud to her in the darkness of his room, "how will the world be without you? How will this city alter if you are no longer here? Will you leave stains of yourself around, or will I be the only one who remembers you? Perhaps I alone shall bear witness of your existence, and I'll remember the joy that I gave you" (for she very much seemed to be the type of girl who would be delighted at unexpected presents), " and I will know you smiled for me alone."

What a pleasing thought. What a fantastic, warming idea that is. He hugged her smile close to him, happy that he was going to please her before he owned her. She would be his favorite butterfly in a jar.

He knew she would simply adore his gift. He would make sure it would be the best, most superb gift that she ever received.

How to do that, he wondered? What is it about a gift that makes it so incredibly memorable?

Ah, that's right. It is all in the packaging.

Chapter Twenty Three
A Brief Essay on Gifts

There are few people who are not genuinely delighted when it comes to gifts.

Whether you are giving them or receiving them, there is something undeniably magic that skitters up one's spine and makes one shiver in anticipation. A gift! A surprise! Something unexpected and shiny and sparkly where before there was . . . nothing! Suddenly there is something new to squirrel away and whisper to in the dark, quiet parts of the evening.

And when one gives a gift, one is transformed from Billy Next Door to A Generous Benefactor, and when the receiver opens their box, they are full of gratitude and awe for the kindness and insight of the giver, who knew exactly what they wanted.

Unless, of course, it is a particularly terrible gift that is delivered in an undeniably ill-chosen fashion. And it is a sorrowful thing to say, but that is exactly what happened with the murderer and his carefully chosen gift for Bryony.

The gift itself was a charming thing, a delicate star on a chain that inspires whimsy and sparkly rainbows of happiness, but that wasn't the problem. The problem was where the murderer found it. It was a trophy he had taken home from an earlier kill—a rather mannish brunette with a penchant for fine things. And after she had been stashed away in several places across the valley, he placed this necklace along with the others in his stash.

Oh, he had beads and rings and a tongue bar, and even the gruesome second joint of a woman's pinky finger he had a special fondness for, though even he couldn't explain it.

But the young girl on the trail, the one who radiated her own soft light, needed stars, and a star he had, and he was quite certain the earlier owner wouldn't put up a fuss if her necklace was passed along to somebody else, somebody a little more deserving, and—dare he say it?— a little livelier than her. Really, wouldn't it be quite selfish of the muscular brunette to begrudge a thing of such beauty to the glowing girl on the trail? After all, she wasn't using it, and would never use it again, this much was certain.

Now the murderer was left to ponder the exact way he should get the wondrous gift to the girl. After all, if he were to simply hand her a creatively wrapped package and say: "Hello, dear girl, I am the man who shall be the death of you, but first I would like to present you with this trinket in order to commemorate the event. I do hope that you like it. See? It's shiny!" Well, then. She would look at him askance and bound off to the nearest police station, and his life would certainly change, and most likely not for the better.

So that was right out.

But he wanted something that would really make

an impression; something that she could reflect on for years to come, or at least, for the rest of her life, which he was fairly certain wouldn't stretch as long.

He considered himself a patient man for the most part, but didn't think he could wait that long. He wanted his hands around her throat, his teeth on the back of her neck, the knife zipping along in its usual friendly, productively busy manner.

Bzzzzzzz, it would hum as he slid it between bones and joints and across the fluid surface of her skin. Did she have tattoos, he wondered? He so hoped she had a discreet tattoo hidden away from the eye of Every-Day Every-Man, a tattoo that he would be able to study and feel and eventually cut away, and frame as art. Yes.

But he digresses. He will save that luscious thought for later, and instead focus on the subject at hand. The gift and its packaging, and the ever-so-sticky problem of delivery.

He clicked his tongue and thought of the things he knew about her; her tendency to be gregarious and the way her soul washed out on the waves as she stared at the water after a tough run.

Ah, yes. How perfect, truly.

He would be able to combine pleasing the Star Girl with his first love, which of course is the stalking, the waiting, and the almost unbearable pleasure of hearing his victim gasp and fight, and eventually the consuming silence that occurs afterward. That silence, untouched by breath, unstained by the constant beat, beat, beating of a heart hidden under clothes and skin and ribs and tissue.

Oh. There is nothing quite like it on this earth.

It is time. It is time.

The murderer scooped the star necklace into his pocket, ran a comb through his dark hair, and set out into the fine, fine evening.

Chapter Twenty Four
Eddie on Edge

Eddie didn't sleep that night.

This was for many reasons.

One, he was extremely nervous about playing at the station in the morning. Had he chosen the right songs? Would Bryony be moved by the one he had written especially for her, the one teased from Jasmine the Guitar on that fine, moon-magic evening? He had never played it for her before, and he could imagine her eyes growing starry and luminous with her joy, and hoped she would be bouncing eagerly from foot to foot, impatient to hug him, impatient to cover the bottom half of his face with kisses, ready to slip her anxious hand into his as she stood stalwart beside him. There would be interviews and maybe even autographs, and they would network and make small talk and schmooze, and do all of those necessary, yet sometimes delightful, things of making and selling music.

This was, quite honestly, enough to make him nervous on its own, but something else had Eddie on edge.

It was the feeling of dying, the feeling of: "Oh no, how can I possibly do this again?" that coursed through his veins like love or venom, from time to time. Bryony's siren call for death meant monsters would come, and that's how it would end for her, and he knew it. He felt that perhaps he could withstand a tragic Accident, whether it was a car or fire or a confused-yet-angry bear from the woods. He would stand resolutely by her casket, managing not to shed a tear, as though he had turned to stone inside.

"I'm so sorry that Bryony fell off of the hiking trail and landed in a den of rattlesnakes," somebody would whisper, an old woman, maybe, and she would hug Eddie fiercely, leaving grandma perfume and outdated lipstick on his fine white lapel.

"It is all right," he would answer tersely, although ever polite. "These things happen, you know, and it isn't anybody's fault. It was a terrible, terrible Accident."

And that is how he would comfort himself. If she was eaten by sharks or hit by a meteor, of course he would go through the "If only I hadn't said: 'Yes, Bryony, I do believe you are correct, and today is the day you learn how to hang-glide!' Then surely she would be alive." phase. It would be almost inhuman not to. But at the end, as he curled up with his memories of her, he would be forced to admit he is not a god, and doesn't have power over the universe. If something so unusual were to happen to her, then who is he to stop it? He can't see the future. He can't alter the cosmos. Will that lessen the pain? No, not really, but at least it would be a fluke of the universe, and not something more sinister.

Of course our Eddie is tormented by thoughts of Rita, and the pictures of her body the police shoved in front of him. The things that were done, the liberties that were taken, made him furious, they turned him into the kind of man he never planned to be. A man who hated, a man who hunted something and somebody to better hate.

It's the intent of the thing that really got him.

That a monster sought out a person to hurt. He lay in wait for somebody full of vibrancy and life, and then perversely enjoyed bleeding it out . . . Well, that wasn't right. It was downright *wrong*. And although Eddie was the kind of guy to let people choose their own idea of right and wrong, according to what suited them, he was unafraid to stand up and publicly declare that, hey, killing people was *wrong*, and torture was *wrong*, and pulling the living light out of somebody's eyes for your own enjoyment is *wrong wrong wrong*. He does not try to be judgmental by this; he is simply declaring his own beliefs. And what he believes is this:

If you so much as lay a finger on my Bryony, I will come after you. I will come after you and I will make you pay and you will be sorry until the end of your days because you do not want to experience what will happen to you. You can't do that to her. I won't let you. I won't let you.

So Eddie thought, strumming and fretting.

He practiced his song for Bryony until it was, oh, so perfect, and he feared what he had always feared since he had met her. He feared her death. He feared being lost without her. He feared waking up one morning and realizing that there might not be anything left.

Chapter Twenty Five
A Terrible Smile

*D*addy?"

"Sweetheart. How are you?"

"I miss you, Daddy."

"I miss you, too, sweetie. Is everything all right?"

"I . . . yes, yes, it is. I just want you here more than usual, I suppose. But everything is fine."

"You would tell me if it wasn't, wouldn't you?"

"Of course, Daddy. I just . . . wanted to tell you I'm okay. I love you, and I . . . what's that sound?"

"It's nothing to worry about, honey."

"It's the desert, isn't it? I can hear it even here, over the sound of the water. It sounds so angry."

"It wants you, child, but it can't have you. It's frustrated, but isn't that a beautiful thing? Sometimes I listen to it at night, growling its plans, and it makes me smile. I can feel it on my face, and it's a terrible smile. A smile that I never thought would belong to me, but there it is. It is aching for you, and the frustration that it is exhibiting . . . Well, it's beautiful. It might be one of the best things I have ever heard. The sound of its exasperated yearning? Ah. It makes my heart glad, dear one. It is the sound of you living your life. It is the sound of your survival. It means it hasn't caught you yet, and sometimes I almost believe it never will. I think that it is the most exquisite sound I have ever heard."

Chapter Twenty Six
If Something Were To Happen

Bryony and Rikki-Tikki hardly missed a practice. The sound of her fists rhythmically hitting against his open palms was both soothing and empowering. Sometimes Syrina would come in and watch, and scream: "Go for his eyes, Bryony! This murderer wants to take you down! Go straight for his eyes!", but usually it was just Bryony and her very precious Rikki-Tikki.

"Rikki-Tikki, you have become a brother to me," she told him.

He grinned. "Nothin' like fighting to make you feel like family."

It was the evening before Eddie had to play at the station, and they were having an especially lovely practice with fists and feet, and Bryony's ponytail flying through the air.

In the midst of the delightful mayhem Rikki-Tikki said: "Everybody seems to have been touched by fate so far, except maybe for Eddie. I wonder when his turn will come."

He watched carefully as Bryony's eyes lost their

starlight glimmer and the bones of her face seemed to press against her skin.

"Ah, you almost forgot us," the bones whispered to Rikki-Tikki, "but indeed, here we are. We are death and fragility and decay and we lurk ever so close to the surface. How cunning we are! We ride around inside of Bryony's skin and we are as intertwined with her as murder. There is no escape."

But Bryony didn't stop or flee. She thought of the many people she had lost—of her young friend Samantha Collins' horribly proper funeral, and the way Teddy Baker had broken her heart, and how her darling Jeremy had broken her life, and then she thought of her sweet, sweet, brave and strong Eddie. If something were to happen . . .

"You shall not touch him," she silently warned fate, and the stars on her wrist glittered as she continued to punch and kick with a newly ferocious determination.

Rikki-Tikki nodded his head in satisfaction.

Later at his apartment, he massaged his bruised hands while fate hissed and scrabbled at the window outside.

"She might not beat you," he said aloud, "but she's going down fighting."

Before crawling into bed, he pulled his sparring pads out of the closet. He was going to need them from now on. The girl was blinking the stardust out of her eyes. She was getting good.

Chapter Twenty Seven
All in the Packaging

A fairly decent arrangement, if he had to say so himself. And he did. The pendant was perfectly placed. It was ready.

The murderer took a second longer to admire his work, and then ran. He ran, as the Star Girl ran, running so that he was not caught, running away from what he had done, because somewhere inside he knew he was doing A Bad Thing, and people who do Bad Things are the kind of people who are supposed to run away. Perhaps subconsciously he ran away from Eddie, who was now at this very second threatening anybody who would ever harm or even disturb his Bryony, and the murderer had left the gift in a memorable way, yes, but not a nice way, or even a fairly decent way. In fact, he would upset the Star Girl very much.

Chapter Twenty Eight
The Gift

I found a body in the water this morning," Bryony said to Police Detective Ian Bridger.

He was young, and he tried to seem hard, but somehow he wasn't able to pull it off. He was a sweet man underneath, the kind that called his mama and worked on the neighbors' cars without expecting payment. This was maybe why the girls was able to talk to him so freely when her tongue had frozen up with his partner. His partner had looked right through her, looked at the body as though it was nothing except an annoyance. It wasn't an annoyance; it was a woman. At least it had been. Once.

"Why were you at the lake?" the detective asked her. He spoke softly, afraid that if he raised his voice he would spook this young woman, this poor shuddering girl who had seen such a terrible sight. Her eyes had faded, the irises dimmed from whatever color they had been, to a pale gray. Her pupils seemed to be shaped like stars. Those eyes kept roving to a small cactus sprung up next to the water. Strange that a desert cactus should suddenly grow there, but while the detective was merely curious, this girl looked absolutely haunted by it.

Bryony wished she had a coat to pull around her. She felt bare, as though she wasn't wearing enough to keep herself decent. It was a horrible feeling, a sad and alone type of feeling, and she wondered if she would ever feel fully dressed again.

Detective Bridger didn't look away from her shame, however, but into her eyes, and spoke..

"I went jogging. I usually go jogging, and then I end up watching the water. It feels . . . " She couldn't seem to think of the word and eventually just skipped over it " . . . somehow," she finished, and Detective Bridger nodded. He understood, he was the kind of man who *believes*.

"She was breathtaking," Bryony said. "Ethereal in the water. I felt like I was looking at a sprite. I felt like I was seeing something nobody on earth was allowed to see, and somehow I managed to get a secret glimpse. I have never seen anything so lovely."

The detective looked at her carefully. He was watching all of the thoughts and feelings as they shadowed her face, and they told him more than her words ever could.

"You don't seem to be very surprised," he said.

Bryony laughed and it was a bitter, bitter sound.

"I'm not surprised, not really. These things always seem to happen. It has been this way since I was a girl, so I am used to it. Each time somebody dies, it is sad. Each time somebody runs across bones or hair or somebody's eyes staring into the sky when they don't intend to be staring there . . . it is shocking, just for a second. There is horror, just for a second, and then it all goes back to normality. The rise and fall of life. The sound of breathing, the feel of feet pounding the sidewalk. I realize I am alive, I have cheated through to another day and I am appreciative. Nobody appreciates life quite like I do, detective. (He very much liked the way that she called him "detective". It sounded different than when anybody else, including his wife, did so.) "But it is wearying sometimes, knowing that they died because of me. It is a great responsibility to bear."

Being an astute detective, of course he questioned that. "What do you mean, because of you?"

He did not think she was involved in the murder. She didn't have that way about her, the almost manic undertone to her words many killers possess. She spoke with sorrow, fatigued by the words she had to say. But Detective Bridger was thinking about the eyeless woman, discovered in a dumpster at Safeway, and the scared punk they pulled in for questioning. While the guy burbled about Mountain Dew and something about throwing fish, Detective Bridger worried about the possibility of a serial killer. He thought perhaps the killings might be related to the string of sometimes fatal robberies that had been occurring in the city, but that robber had been put out of commission by a fierce young woman and her saucepan, (and after interviewing her in the hospital, he could easily picture her bloody vengeance) and still the killings continued.

But still, he was a kind man, and being a kind man and a good detective went hand in hand for him, so he had to ask.

Bryony smiled at him then. "Detective, when you look at me, what do you see?"

He thought, Is this a trick question?

He thought, "What a strange thing to ask."

He thought, "I see a lovely young woman, a woman that I wish I had known as a child. She reminds me of somebody I am absolutely certain I have never met. And she is going to die. She is going to die. She is going to wash up on the shores of the lake like this woman here, and somebody is going to find her with her hair waving around her pale face, and her fingers loose in death like they never had the chance to be in life. And somebody is going to identify the body, and when he does his heart is going to break, and I'm going to stand there and watch him silently shatter apart in the way that loved ones do in the face of death. And after he leaves, I am going to stand for a long time looking at the face of this woman, the way that her eyes will gaze at the stars until it is time to pull the sheet over her face, and I won't be able to do it. I simply won't."

Bryony nodded at him. "Exactly," she said. "Exactly. So you know."

And they both cried together.

Chapter Twenty Nine
A Question that is Never Asked

Eddie blew everybody away down at the station, just as he hoped. He was a little upset that Bryony wasn't there like she promised, but he figured she had a good reason. And she did, because when he was nervously strumming the first few words of his new song, she was sobbing into the detective's shoulder, thinking of the life she would never get to live with Eddie.

Too soon. Too soon. It was coming.

The body floating in Lake Washington had been a particularly young and pretty girl whose name is not important. It would have been to her family if they had been aware of her death, but they hadn't been in contact with her for years, ever since she left to run away with a man named Mike. Every girl has dated a Mike in her life, and very few of them have turned out to be a good decision, but it happens. This Mike turned out to be a typical Mike situation, and as soon as the girl told him that she was having a baby, he left her. Now this turned out to be a miscalculation on the girl's part, and there really was no baby, but since she found out the true depth (or lack thereof) of Mike's character, she decided that she was better off without him. As she would have been under most circumstances, but the very sad fact of the matter was that if she had been with Mike that particular night, she most likely would still be alive. So dead and without the roguish Mike, or alive and with him . . . really, either of these two options were undesirable, although one was preferable over the other.

But at the time of her murder, she was Mikeless, in a state of Without Mike, and it was a very simple thing for our murderer to step behind her, bash her in the back of the head, and hold her underwater until her fine existence was finished. A tiny star pendant was affixed to her neck (for Bryony's pale skin simply begged to be adorned with stars), and her body was brought to rest in the water where Bryony would be sure to see her in the early morning. Tomorrow was Wednesday, you know. Several large rocks in her pockets kept her in place so that she did not float away, and after a few exploratory pecks, the ducks left her alone.

And it was done.

The murderer was angry that Bryony did not take the necklace from the girl's neck and put it on her own. He chose it with such care. He presented it with such panache. But after further examination, it made sense and he forgave her. Bryony was a sweet girl, a decent girl, and obviously misunderstood the murderer's intentions. She would most certainly not think to rob the dead, and didn't realize that the gift was expressly for her. Next time it would be made clear.

But that is not the matter that is being discussed, is it? The matter at hand is Eddie. And Eddie was successful at the radio station and unhappy with Bryony.

He found her sitting on the lifeguard's chair, staring at the water. The detectives had long since gone away. The body long since removed.

"I missed you today," Eddie said. His hands were in his pockets, and he was trying to be cordial, trying to be polite in case there was a reason, a very good reason that Bryony wasn't there. He hoped it was the case, that she was busy or had a Very Important Phone Call, or some other valid excuse that kept her when he wanted her there so badly, when so much depended on his intricate playing. For Eddie was quite hurt. As a matter of fact, few things had ever hurt him that much, and at the time he was unable to think of anything else that stung him as badly. The memory of playing her special song and constantly flicking his eyes to the corner of the room to see if she had discreetly crept in, well, it made his cheeks burn. *Bryony better have a good reason,* was all that he could think.

She flew out of the chair and into his arms with so much force that he nearly fell backward.

"Oh, Eddie. I found a body here this morning, floating in the water. Or rather, she found me, and I couldn't leave her here, because she was so alone, you see. I wish that I could have seen you. I am so very proud of you, Eddie, and I hope you aren't angry with me. Today was such an important day, and you have worked so hard for it, but I couldn't leave her here. Her feet were bare and I had never seen toes as vulnerable, and she was so . . . "

She couldn't say any more, and she didn't need to,

because suddenly Eddie knew without a doubt the body was sent there specifically for Bryony, that it was a message, that it was time. It was time to run.

"Bryony," he said, and she looked up with her large eyes. "Pack your clothes. We are going to see your father. Immediately."

Her smile was like the water, courageous with an undercurrent of calm, terrified violence underneath. "We are?"

Her father, hooray!

But the desert was another matter.

She pushed her hair out of her face and the stars around her wrist glittered. Eddie suddenly knew they were being watched right now and he couldn't deny it even if he wanted to. Of course, he would deny for the sake of tough, masculine appearances because underneath his creativity, Eddie really was a sensible man.

"We are," he said, and held her close. This was the way it was supposed to be, and he knew it, and suddenly it seemed silly to even pretend otherwise.

"Bryony, when we see your father . . . " He didn't know what to say. Shouldn't this come easy? Shouldn't he have thought of it in advance? Shouldn't this a luminous and a shining moment that they would both remember forever?

Her eyes. Her eyes. She looked at him and took him apart piece by piece and put him back together as something better than he had ever been before. She was everything he had ever needed, and suddenly he realized with perfect clarity he was everything she had ever needed, too. He couldn't be any more perfect to her. If she could have anything in the entire world, anything at all, she would stand right there with her perfect eyes and she would say in a calmly determined voice, "I would like Eddie Warshouski, please."

"Yes," he said to her.

"Yes?" she asked him. She held onto his hands as tightly as she possibly could, and yet her little hands were so fragile. Bird bones, tiny ribbons of calcium. He could smash them so easily. Anyone could.

"Yes, and yes, and yes," he said again, urgently. Tonight, if they could, but it would only be proper to marry with her father there, and anything else would greatly devastate the man's feelings.

"Really?" she asked, and she glowed. Nuclear happiness, delight ascending. He expected light to shoot from her fingers and toes, but no, it only shimmered under the surface of her skin.

"I love you," he said. In those words was everything else he meant, things like: Why waste time? And: Why did it ever take me so long to figure it out? And: I will miss you so very much when you are gone, it will devastate me. He also thought: *I am marrying the stars and I have never been so happy. Ha, take that, Chad the Fish guy, it sucks to be you.* There was a myriad of other things he thought about, too.

"I love you," is all that Eddie actually uttered, and somehow those words were enough.

"When are we leaving?" asked a radiant Bryony.

"Right now, love," Eddie answered.

He grabbed her hand and they ran across the grass and to the parking lot, laughing.

The murderer wasn't laughing. This was an unfortunate turn of events, for these things are much harder to carry out with a doting man in tow, especially one that is stealing the Star Girl's exceptional smiles. If there is one thing that is true, though, it is that if you really want something badly enough, it is always possible.

And it is true. It is true.

Unless, unfortunately, your name is Bryony Adams and what you want is to live.

Chapter Thirty
Child of the Sky

Detective Bridger sat at his desk with several grisly pictures spread out in front of him. Lovely young women without heads, without hands, without eyes. Women with their heads shaved and women with their bodies disassembled. There didn't seem to be anything in particular linking them together, but the sheer number of victims caught his attention, and the sadness around their tender mouths kept it.

How many mothers will pick up the phone to call their daughters, and then suddenly sink into a chair when they remember nobody will answer? How many little girls will grow up without somebody's gentle hands braiding their hair? What the good detective didn't want to admit to anybody, especially himself, was that whenever he closed his eyes he saw Bryony Adams' face staring up at him from each portrait.

Bryony devoid of skin and clothing and emotion. Bryony imperceptibly shaking her head and saying, "Why didn't you help me, Detective Bridger? Why did you let me slip away from this world when you took one look at me and you *knew*?"

The current victims were heart wrenching, but how much worse will Bryony's death be because he knew ahead of time, and was unable to stop it?

He knew instinctively that when the moment came, when this child of the sky was murdered and left lying in a broken heap of muscle and bone and tissue somewhere, the stars would darken and life would not be nearly as beautiful as it was before.

He had to save her. He had to try.

Chapter Thirty One
The Desert is Waiting

Syrina and Rikki-Tikki were, of course, thrilled with the news that Bryony and Eddie were getting married. Syrina immediately dumped her coffee can of spare change out on the bed, but it wasn't nearly enough to buy a plane ticket. She pouted briefly but was quickly caught up again in the splendid rush of excitement.

"When?" Syrina asked, helping Bryony throw her meager belongings in a pleasingly large suitcase. "When is the wedding?"

"Hopefully tonight," Bryony said, "although it is more likely that we'll get married tomorrow. I have to be realistic, you know."

"Yes, indeed you do," Syrina agreed. "That's my girl. How I wish we could come. But here, wear this dress and think of me at least once during the ceremony. It will look stunning!"

They discussed the big party they would throw when Eddie and Bryony came back, and what kind of delicious treats they should have, and how Bryony should wear her hair for the wedding. Up, it was decided. Wearing your hair up meant fine things, such as in the time of balls and galas with lords and ladies. But not harshly up, because Bryony was Bryony. There needed to be room for her hair to have its freedom.

"Where are you going to get married?" Syrina asked her. "Not out in the desert, I hope?"

Being a good and caring roommate, she knew all about Bryony's fears, and how the desert longed to scrape its left fang down her femur, and what a terrible brute it had always been.

"My first thought is no," said Bryony, "but perhaps that wouldn't be a bad idea. To cancel out the desert with a wedding, something wonderful and amazing. To blot out the blackness with a thing of beauty. I wonder what Eddie will say?"

Back at his apartment, Eddie was making a rushed phone call to his mother while packing.

"Hi, Ma, it's me. Things are going great, thanks. Hey, I wanted to tell you that . . . no, I didn't see that news story on TV. Tell me all about it in a minute, Ma, because . . . oh, uh huh. Uh huh."

Mrs. Warshouski lived back in Iowa and enjoyed a quieter kind of life there, although she tended to fill it with drama about who was dating who in the cul de sac, and the rising price of dairy products, and all of the child predators showing up repeatedly on Dateline, fairly *knowing* they were being lured into a trap but plunging along headfirst anyway. However today she was telling Eddie about an especially aggressive type of insect that was attacking her roses and it was of great concern to her, and she would not rest, no, not one *second* until this hated insect was no longer at large.

"Ma, I'm getting married," Eddie finally broke in when his mother paused for breath. After he said that, there was a longer, greater pause. Mrs. Warshouski seemed to have forgotten how to breathe, stunned with Eddie's rather impromptu and delightfully mystifying announcement. So, Eddie hoped.

"Is that true, Eddie? Really, for real?"

"Really for real," he said.

To Eddie's relief, there was much screaming and laughter and hopping up and down on both sides of the phone, and a good time was had by all while they relished this moment. Eddie threw socks and his razor and a clean pair of jeans into his backpack as he told his mother all about Bryony. He told her what Bryony looked like and the almost tinkling sound of her voice, and her habit of standing on the balls of her feet when she gets nervous because somehow that puts her in touch with the earth a little bit more.

"You'll love her, Ma, you'll love her," he said, and promised to bring her by soon so they could meet. He was afraid, however, that the second his mother saw Bryony, her face would fall. He imagined her brown eyes clouding over as she pulled his new wife into her arms, holding her close and whispering: "Oh darling, oh my beautiful baby girl, how could life do this to you? How could anybody? It isn't fair."

Perhaps she would, because Mrs. Warshouski was a kind soul. That much was apparent by the good and fine way her son chose to conduct himself, even after spending several years outside the bosom of home. But Mrs. Warshouski is also a woman of spunk and will. It would be unfair if it wasn't at least mentioned, and who knows, perhaps she would storm right up to fate, kick it smartly in the shin and say: "Oh, don't you so much as dare look at us strangely, you naughty thing, for I simply won't have it. I demand a fine quality of life for my son and that girl and I will not *stand* for you to hover around them in such a distressing manner. Now be off with you!"

Would this tactic have worked? What a delightful notion to entertain the possibility that it might have been the very thing that would send fate a-packing. Fate is a pushy thing of late, arrogant and sure of itself because it is seldom challenged, and it naturally assumes it can roll over everything and everyone in its way. What a bully fate has become.

But do not underestimate the mother of Eddie Warshouski, oh no, because she might come out on top, and it would certainly be a struggle to watch, wouldn't it? Who would you place your bets on?

The unfortunate truth is we will never get to witness the grand grudge match that would have gone on between Mrs. Warshouski and fate. Eddie's mother never receives the opportunity to meet Bryony, and it is a sad thing, and an unfair one, but that is the way that these scenes play out sometimes.

There was a murder, you see, and this murder ends something that could have been beautiful, as murders often tend to do.

Chapter Thirty Two
The Horror of Love

Daddy, this is Eddie. I love him, and he loves me, and he is strong enough to handle anything that needs handling, and you'd better listen carefully because now I'm going to be Mrs. Warshouski. That's W-a-r-s-h-o-u-s-k-i. Warshouski. Now let's get everybody together because we really would like to get married soon, please."

Bryony threw herself onto her aging father, who cried happy tears for his little girl. And Eddie reached out to shake his hand, but he was drawn into the hug, as well, and Stop kept saying: "Bless you, my boy."

Eyes were wet and smiles were genuine and Eddie looked around the house and deemed Bryony's childhood home to be absolutely lovely and worthy of her.

Then he turned and looked out of the window
toward
the
desert.

"It has always been this way," Bryony offered by way of explanation, and Eddie had to go and sit down for a minute because his heart threatened to stop and his legs tried to give out.

"How can you live in such a place?" he asked Bryony's father, who watched him with quiet eyes. "It wants her so badly, and is so angry. Doesn't it feel like it wants to consume you, too, just because you are so close to her?"

"It does," Stop said, and he sat stiffly into a chair next to Eddie. Eddie reached out to massage the kink out of the old man's right leg, and Stop smiled at him. "It is angry and will always be angry, I think, until it gets her. But it won't get her, not now. Not here. She has fled from it, and doesn't belong to it anymore. It writhes and hisses and screams, and this leads me to believe that she belongs to a different fate now."

Bryony watched Eddie's face. She was certain he thought about the eyes he felt on the running trail, and about the unlucky women who had gone missing from the area. Death can be such a gruesome transformation.

A girl disappears, and a body turns up in her place, bereft and without soul. It is not a fair trade, not in the least, but that is exactly how it happens. There are bodies in the woods, bodies in the dumpsters. Bodies hidden in crawl spaces and in the trunks of cars and tossed into ravines. Bodies floating in the water and bodies with a thin skiff of dirt on top. They are soaked by the constant, weeping rain, not the strong desert rain Bryony had experienced, but a creeping, mewling rain. They are blanched and stepped over, and apple cores are hurled nearby. People, out walking their dogs, stumble upon them, this almost self-sustaining plethora of bodies

Bryony kissed her father on his cheek and then Eddie on his. "Why worry about this now? Daddy, Eddie and I have decided we would like to get married in the desert."

There was silence, as she knew there would be, and Stop's mind whirred, as she knew it would. She waited while he thought through scenarios and made decisions, and schemes and plans and then scrapped them all and began anew. Finally he nodded his head, and Bryony nodded with him, and the decision was made, precisely as Bryony had explained to Eddie it would happen.

"Yes," Stop said slowly. "That is fitting. When would you like this to occur?"

Eddie and Bryony looked at each other and smiled, and Stop smiled, too, and there was a flurry of phone calls and little children running up and down the street to tell the news, and within two hours everybody in the town was cleaned and pressed and gathered out into the heart of the desert for the sacred and joyful occasion.

The minister, who was a very sweet man who milked the town's three cows every morning, smiled at Bryony and shook Eddie's hand firmly up and down. "You couldn't be luckier," he said, and Eddie agreed wholeheartedly. "You couldn't be luckier."

Bryony had a cactus flower in her hair, a striking red against her pale hair and skin. "Fie!" the desert cried when the flower was picked. "I refuse to be adornment for the one who I have yet to claim. The nerve. I shall hex you all at once!" But the desert can rant and rave all it wants, in the end it is still only terrain. The flower was plucked and nestled gently into

Bryony's smooth hair, and the irony was not lost on anybody.

Bryony looked around and her eyes filled with tears.

Everybody she had known growing up, give or take a soul or two, was there. She saw Samantha's father and gave him a hug, remembering her friend's pink casket and lackluster funeral. They never found her killer, but that is the way the world works sometimes, and he cried bitterly as he held Bryony and thought of his daughter and the wedding she would never enjoy. She saw the dear old women who had mother-henned her after her own mother abandoned her, she saw the old butcher who used to horrify the town's children with obscure cuts of bloodied meat. And she saw Teddy Baker, he who first broke her heart. He stood there with his wife and their baby girl, and they smiled so happily at her that she had to smile back.

None of Teddy's old high school friends came to the wedding, for various reasons. Two were dead, and the rest were in jail, all except one who was now an ophthalmologist in Michigan. Four of them succeeded in getting together one night, and at long last killing a young girl that they met at a rather wild party filled with all manner of unmentionable activities, and although it succeeded in quenching their exploratory curiosity about murder, the girl ended up in parts and the boys ended up in prison, so really nothing was won by this.

Teddy had a tiny daughter now, and had told her the story once of how he had single handedly saved Bryony's life at the expense of her tender feelings. He had wondered aloud what would have happened if he had made the choice to call Bryony his own, and to stand up to his friends, constantly placing himself between fate and her soft flesh, and how they could have lived their life out together in happiness, perhaps.

Only it was never to be so. He had whispered to his baby that he wasn't strong enough, and he knew he would have been worn down by the unyielding terror of the waiting and the fear of her tragic loss. He would have been a ground down shell of a man by the time that her death finally rolled around. Deep inside he felt what would have been the horror of love, and the sickening thought that perhaps he would have welcomed her death, even invited it, if it meant release from the constantly sharp edge of waiting.

He had confessed he was terrified that he, who could have been the loving husband of Bryony Adams Baker, would have finally snapped under the pressure and taken a knife to the throat of his darling wife, releasing first her and then himself from the weighty, oppressive shadow of fate. Who would have found them, he wondered? Who would have walked into their house and eventually their room, and found two blank eyed corpses, but hopefully they would have realized the relief, the relief of being free? Their hands would have been entwined, he just knew it.

Still, Teddy watched carefully as Eddie's eyes darted around the desert and he put his arm protectively around Bryony, and he couldn't help but remember. He remembered that first sweet kiss, and his ensuing distance from the Star Girl afterwards, but he always held close to his heart the secret he had kept. That he had single handedly saved Bryony's life at the expense of her tender feelings. As he cuddled his own tiny daughter, he once again closed his eyes in relief at his decision so long ago. If only some high school boy would be so kind to his little girl when the time came. If only she, too, could live, hopefully forever. He opened his eyes and caught Bryony's.

For a brief instant, he allowed himself to wonder what would have happened if he had made the choice to call Bryony his own, and to stand up to his friends, constantly placing himself between fate and her soft flesh, and how they could have lived their life out together in happiness, perhaps.

Only it was never to be so. Teddy wasn't strong enough, and he knew he would have been worn down by the unyielding terror of the waiting and the fear of her tragic loss. He would have been a ground down shell of a man by the time that her death finally rolled around. Deep inside he felt what would have been the horror of their love, and the sickening thought that perhaps he would have welcomed her death, even invited it, if it meant release from the constantly sharp edge of waiting.

He was terrified that he, who could have been the loving husband of Bryony Adams Baker, would have finally snapped under the pressure and taken a knife to the throat of his darling wife, releasing first her and then himself from the weighty, oppressive shadow of fate. Who would have found them, he wondered? Who would have walked into their house and eventually their room, and found two blank eyed corpses, but hopefully they would have realized the relief, the relief of being free? Their hands would have been entwined, he just knew it.

Bryony, standing beside her groom, looked at

Teddy almost like she knew what he was thinking, and they stood there for a second, frozen in a moment of time that nobody else shared, just the two of them alone.

Teddy dropped his eyes to the ground, and his wife took their fussy daughter and he was alone.

Bryony watched him for a second more before turning back to the minister.

"We are gathered here today," he said, and as he continued, there was a happy shuffling of feet. Bryony Adams was getting married today. All was right with the world.

A snaky desert vine zipped its way across the sand, heading for her exposed ankle. The town butcher stomped on it with his feet, and the vine lay still. Scorpions and crawlies and all manner of dangerous creatures infested the dunes, but they were effectively stamped out and killed by the townsfolk.

"You simply shan't have her tonight," whispered a doddering old woman, a bit too loudly, mind you, but she was a kind and gentle thing, and those around her nodded in agreement. The desert recoiled in disbelief, but pressed on in its advances, only to be stymied at every turn. What a distressing turn of events for the desert at large.

Ah, but what an evening for Bryony!

Her eyes shone, full of Eddie Warshouski and everything he was. Her father stood beside her, and those she loved surrounded him. The moon was bright and large as it can only be in an unbroken sky, and the stars . . . Why, the stars were absolutely spectacular. They erupted in a meteor shower, falling down to the earth around them, coursing across the sky in a sea of white sparks. They were sky confetti, and celebrated the "I do's" and the "You may kiss the bride" and they were positively dazzling when Eddie picked Bryony up and spun her around under the clear atmosphere. She laughed and the stars answered, and it seemed as though they were in her hair and on her eyelashes, and shining under her long white dress. There was much oohing and aahing and happy tears from all involved, and Stop's stooped shoulders were petted and patted and his lined face hurt from smiling so hard.

"This is exactly right," he said. "Exactly right."

And everybody agreed, except for the desert, who was pouting off by itself in a most unflattering manner.

But the desert had a trick up its sleeve, oh yes it did. For it may be thwarted at the moment, but it will not be thwarted for long, and even now there was a rumbling deep underground that made the desert cease feeling sorry for itself. In fact, it began to smile, a harsh smile, a terrible smile, and anybody who witnessed it certainly would have been frozen in horror, pierced by the chill one feels when they drop something fragile, something that was given to them by somebody very dear who is now dead, and now they have nothing with which to remember them, and shall never be able to recall their features exactly ever again.

Chapter Thirty Three
Are You Alive? Here Are Some Muffins

Detective Bridger stood outside the door for a second before knocking. He felt rather silly holding a basket of warm muffins, but his wife had insisted. The detective cleared his throat and tried to look extra official.

Rikki-Tikki answered the door. "Yes?"

The detective's eyes narrowed. "What are you doing here?"

"Good to see you again, Detective Bridger. How's our homicidal home invader?"

Detective Bridger smiled slightly. "I think that particular man is scared straight for a good long while. He didn't want to confess to any of the other crimes until we threatened to put him in a locked room with Syrina. Suddenly he had a lot to say."

"She'll be pleased to hear that. What can I do for you, detective?"

Detective Bridger straightened. "I was looking for Miss Adams. I was going to . . . my wife . . . these muffins," he said awkwardly, and held them out to Rikki-Tikki.

"She isn't home right now."

"When will she be back?"

"Not for a while."

Detective Bridger stared at Rikki-Tikki and Rikki-Tikki stared right back. High in the trees a blackbird eyed the muffins greedily, but its sense of self-preservation convinced it to stay away. It flew off with shiny-eyed disappointment.

"Isn't it unusual for a detective to show up at a young girl's house with breakfast?" Rikki-Tikki asked.

Detective Bridger straightened. "I don't appreciate your implication. I'm checking up on her to see how she was doing after finding that body. She seemed to be quite devastated by it."

"You wanted to reassure yourself that she was still alive."

Detective Bridger ignored this, although it was precisely that.

Rikki-Tikki held his hand out for the muffins and Detective Bridger passed them over automatically. Rikki-Tikki could see he was busy fitting the pieces of the puzzle together.

"You're wondering if the attack on Syrina had anything to do with Bryony. It did. You realize that Bryony is somewhat of . . . a target."

Detective Bridger's eyes sharpened on Rikki-Tikki's. "I can't say it's something I understand, but I can't deny what I felt when I saw her. She is followed by sorrow. But are you saying that the rest of you suffer consequences for being so close to her?"

Rikki-Tikki took a bite of muffin. "I wouldn't call it

suffering. We hold our own." He swallowed. "She's gone home for a few days. Getting married to Eddie."

"Who's Eddie?"

"Ed Warshouski. He's a musician."

The detective sighed and Rikki-Tikki thought he didn't look as severely official as he had before. He looked like somebody who played ball and ate chicken wings and would be fun to hang out with during weekends.

"Eddie Warshouski. I remember his case. They make a pair," Detective Bridger said. "Good luck to the both of them. I'm afraid they'll need it."

He turned to go but Rikki-Tikki put a hand on his shoulder.

"Hey, Detective."

"Yes?"

Rikki-Tikki leaned against the door. "You're all right. You genuinely want to help our Bryony."

"Of course I do. Why wouldn't I?"

Rikki-Tikki's grin looked strangely ghostly, and for a second the detective could see a trace of Bryony in that smile. When she was lost (and yes, he would work as diligently as it is humanly possible for a man to work, but the fact of the tragic matter is that she will indeed be lost), Detective Bridger will comfort himself knowing that on sad, rather melancholy days, Rikki-Tikki will smile a rather dismal smile and there will be, at least for a second, a trace of the Star Girl.

"You'd be amazed at all of the predators in the world," Rikki-Tikki said off-handedly. "But I want to tell you this: If you continue to help her, you're putting yourself and your family in danger."

Detective Bridger's voice was calm. "Is that a threat?"

Rikki-Tikki's grin brightened, and all of the world was filled with sun. "No, it's a very friendly warning. I thought you deserved to hear it. Welcome to our team, Detective Bridger."

He shut the door and the detective stood silently for a minute, piecing everything together in his head. His heart was pounding a bit quicker as he walked briskly back to the car.

Chapter Thirty Four
Pain and Peace

Today was a beautiful day as far as Mrs. Warshouski was concerned. Her darling Eddie was getting married, and what could possibly be better than that? Why, nothing. Nothing. Soon their house would be full of tiny Edwards and . . . what was her name again? A poisonous flower. Oleander? Baneberry? Goodness, that can't be it. No mother in her right mind would ever name her daughter Baneberry.

Mrs. Warshouski could just see it now . . .

"Why, hello, new mother. I am your nurse. You have a tiny baby girl."

"Oh, do I? How utterly delightful. I am ever so happy."

"As am I. What a pleasure to assist in the labor and delivery. And what, pray tell, are you going to name your little bundle of goodness and light?"

"I shall call her Baneberry."

" . . . Shall you? Oh my."

"Yes. I wish to give my daughter a rather conflicting name, you see, and I felt that being called after a poisonous flower would do just that. First I thought of Elephant Ear, but you can imagine how that would be when she hits twelve or so—"

"Yes, yes, I see your point," the nurse would whisper ever so faintly.

"And there are so many other names to choose from, really. Gardenia and Foxglove. False Hellebore is just right out, you see, but Baneberry . . . "

Mrs. Warshouski shook her head to take the image from her mind. What a terrible fate to befall such a sweet girl. Thank goodness her mother had chosen to call her . . . ooh, if only she could remember.

It is quite an unusual name, she consoled herself as she bustled around the house. One day it will roll off her tongue like pearls, and she and her daughter-in-law will laugh and laugh about how Mrs. Warshouski was quite befuddled over the name, and couldn't remember it to save her life.

"Oh, Mama, you are ever so funny," the dear girl would say, and kiss Mrs. Warshouski's cheek. She did hope the child chose to call her Mama, especially after Eddie told her the poor thing didn't have a mother of her own. Mrs. Warshouski was enough mother to mother them both, and by golly, that was what she was going to do.

She flung open the windows to the upstairs guest room, letting the night freshen the air. Although she was not quite well enough to board one of those horrid airplanes and traverse the country to attend a last minute wedding. Mrs. Warshouski had asked Eddie, without being pushy, if he and his darling new bride would be willing to come and stay with her so they could enjoy each other's company.

"You just want to scope her out, don't you, Ma?" Eddie teased. Before she even had a chance to chide him for being cheeky, he said: "Of course we'll be there. I can't wait for you to meet her, Ma. You'll love her. And she'll be just wild about you, I guarantee it."

What a nice boy, a sweet boy. A gentle boy who thought about his mother and knew that more than anything she wanted to be liked and accepted by his wife. She wanted to be a part of the family and spend time with the couple, and hold all of their sweet babies. She knew there would be babies, and lots of them, and there would be laughter and joy and frantic phone calls where her charming new daughter would say a bit breathlessly: "Oh, Mama, the little tiger is teething and I have no idea what to do. What is your advice? What do you suggest?" And they would discuss, and she would dispense her sage advice, and the girl would nod on her end of the phone. Then she would say: "Yes, oh yes, that makes so much sense! Thank you. When can you come and visit us?" and they would plan Christmases and Easters and leisurely summer vacations together. It will be splendid.

"My heart . . . is full," she said aloud, and it sounded exactly right. She chose to say it again. "My heart is full."

So pleased and full of heady dreams was our precious woman that she didn't even hear the slight sounds were coming from the ground floor of her home. There was the sound of sliding and something tipping over and being gratefully caught at the last minute, and the sound of somebody breathing through their mouth because they were too panicked to breathe through their nose. There was the sound of feet trying their hardest to sound stealthy and the sound of precious-looking things being slid neatly into a backpack. If Mrs. Warshouski would have been thinking about the weather, perhaps, or the Current State of the Economy, it is quite likely she would have been eagerly brought back to reality by such sounds. But alas, she was thinking Happy Thoughts, and Happy Thoughts have a way of inhabiting your mind and soul the same way joyful music or a parasite does, and she was not aware of the oddly peculiar sounds at all. And the creator of the mysterious downstairs sounds was obviously not that aware, either, because he was most surprised when Mrs. Warshouski burst into the room he was currently robbing.

"Oh dear," said Mrs. Warshouski. There was a red headed boy with freckles and frightened green eyes staring at her in surprise. He had a beautiful mouth and her mother's wedding ring in his hands.

"You weren't supposed to be home," he told her. His hand shook, and he slipped the ring into his backpack. He pulled a gun awkwardly out of his waistband.

"Well, I am. I'm sorry; I didn't realize I was supposed to be somewhere else."

Mrs. Warshouski is a polite woman, a woman who chooses to always think the best of others, and as an end result, she simply could not believe this freckled young lad was training a gun on her. Why, it simply wouldn't do. Where is the respect he should be showing her? At the same time, her mind ducked low and wrapped its arms around itself protectively.

"I'm going to have to shoot you, ma'am. I'm sorry of it, I really am, but I can't have you telling my mother or the police."

The young man went deathly white under his freckles, and something in this jogged Mrs. Warshouski's brain.

"Ah, Bryony!" she sighed, and the gun went off, and she clutched at her heart and fell to the ground quite heavily. Something snapped underneath her, and there was so much pain and redness and the terrified face of the young wild boy, but there was also peace.

Bryony. Bryony. That was her name. Ah, yes. What joy. What happiness.

Chapter Thirty Five
If You Had Never Met Me

The phone was ringing back at Stop's home. It rang for several minutes, silenced itself long enough to take a breath, and then rang again. Stop hobbled into the house, cheeks still glowing from the wedding. Bryony and Eddie were close behind.

"Hello?" Stop said into the phone. His voice was merry and young, and it reminded Bryony of when she was a child. Stop used to rollerskate with her. He taught her how to climb trees. "Yes, he's right here. Hold on a second."

He handed the phone to Eddie. Eddie grinned at him.

"Yeah?" he said.

He didn't speak for a long time after that, just listened. His face went paler and paler until he rivaled Bryony herself. She pulled a chair over to him and he sat down.

That's when she knew.

Stop must have realized it, too, because he put his arms around his daughter, smoothing her hair. "It's not your fault, sweetheart. It's not your fault." His newfound youthfulness was a lie, a dreadful deceit, for he was an old man, and old men cannot always hold back their tears. They ran down his face, and Bryony hugged him with all her strength before she went to stand behind her new husband of less than fifteen minutes.

"Thank you," he said faintly into the phone, and Bryony took it from him and hung it up gently. She knelt in front of him and put her hand on his cheeks.

"Eddie," she said softly. "Tell me."

The words were almost more than he could say, but Eddie is a strong man. A brave man and he wanted to do what was right, even if it was difficult. He swallowed and tried to give voice to his mother's spirit.

"My mother. Back home. The neighbor . . . found her." Bryony gasped, but Eddie continued speaking. "There was a robbery, and she must have walked in on him. He has already confessed, this kid. He's just a kid, looking for money. My mother . . . " Tears ran down his face, then, and Bryony climbed into his lap and her starry bracelet shimmered as she threw her arms around him. "She's dead, Bryony. She's dead. We were getting married, and she . . . "

"Oh, Eddie. I'm so sorry. If only you hadn't met me, Eddie. It's a horrible thing to say, but it's true, and we both know it. If only I had gone somewhere else, picked a different market to wander through that day. If only I hadn't chased you down with those yellow jonquils and demanded to know why you didn't like me! Oh, Eddie, you didn't like me at all, and that was a hurtful thing to me, but it was safe for you. Perhaps I should have let it be, because then your mother—"

He tried to say consoling things but was too

distraught, and she tried to say equally consoling things, but was even more distraught. Stop quietly stepped out of the door and stood on the back porch, giving them time to grieve.

The desert laughed.

Stop heard it, and it was a sickly sound, a dark and ancient sound. It sounded even older than Stop felt, and it hardly seemed possible.

"You wicked, hateful thing," he said aloud. His bones felt like they would powder right there as he stood, and the desert would lap them up and mix them with its sand. It would create a golem Stop, and nobody would know the difference, except maybe for Bryony, and she wasn't long for this world either. "You're nothing but spite and malice. You are an evil, evil old horror."

The desert laughed and laughed. The sound made Stop shiver.

Inside young Eddie and his broken bride still cried.

Chapter Thirty Six
He Has a Name

The murderer was thrilled to see Bryony back on the trail. It had been a few days, not so long, as he was beginning to despair of ever seeing her again, but long enough that he had killed twice more in her absence. Nobody spectacular or even very special; just some random people he deemed suitable. But now she was back and ready to play.

Only . . . only there was something different about her, and he couldn't quite figure it out. Something about the way she held herself, something about the shape of her mouth.

Ah, yes. Grief.

How unusual. She was a woman born of grief, and yet somehow she was breaking under the weight of it. It was a lovely thing to see, actually, like the branches of a tree snapping under an ice storm, a sort of beauty in the pale horror of the event, but at the same time, he didn't enjoy seeing her suffer. She moved him in a way he hadn't often been moved. It was like watching a ghost fade away after you had just grown accustomed to it. It was a difficult thing.

Well. He would see what he could do.

"Excuse me, miss," he said, jogging up to her. He made a show of stretching his muscles and kicking around in place for a bit to demonstrate he really had been jogging for a long time, and had not been lurking behind the blackberry bushes like some pervert.

She looked up in surprise, her shoelaces still in her hands. "Why, hello. Can I help you?"

He was a familiar man, one she had seen every now and then as she ran past. His hair looked like it was combed very neatly just before his run, and he seemed to have an exorbitant amount of energy, judging by the way he leapt and bounced all across the trail.

The murderer/jogger man grinned in what he calculated to be a disarming way. "I was just wondering if you could tell me the time. I have an appointment to get ready for and I forgot to bring my watch." That works, he thought. Believable, friendly but not creepy. At least he hoped. Totally not creepy, right?

The girl shielded her eyes from the sun with her hand, and a slender ring of stars ran around her wrist. "I'm sorry, I don't wear a watch," she said, "but I'd guess that it's about . . . oh, I don't know. About seven now? Seven oh five?"

She was right, actually. He had glanced at his watch quickly before tossing it in the bushes.

"What makes you say that?" he asked curiously.

She smiled, just for him, and something inside of him puffed up in joy. He knew he could do it. He knew it! All of these years he feared his lack of talent, his ultimate *ordinariness*, and now he finds he can make this stunning stunning being feel something—peace or joy or safety or whatever she might be feeling—enough that her sorrow can fall from her body like ancient metal armor, and she can actually smile.

"It's the light," she said. "This is seven o' clock light, still filtered and the air is full of mist. It'll burn off soon, and the light will become clearer. I can just usually tell."

"You're beautiful," he said.

"I'm sorry, what was that?"

"Nothing. I just said 'I'm grateful.' Okay, thanks a lot!"

He bounded uncreepily away, resisting the urge to glance back and see if the girl was still watching him. He was almost certain that was the case, and he didn't want to look like an idiot. He put his eyes on the prize, so to speak, and kept up a great, impressive pace until he turned the corner of the trail and disappeared from sight. Then he ducked into the bushes again.

Our murderer was not a runner, not really. He was built for speed, and a little bit for strength, but not really for endurance. That didn't matter much anyway, since he tended to pop out and surprise his victims instead of chasing them down the street like a brain dead Neanderthal. Really. Did people actually still do that these days? Wasn't it the 21st Century?

Still, he did hunt on the trail, and he did spend a lot of time in his carefully chosen running shorts and a shirt that wicked away perspiration. He quite enjoyed reading the labels on these clothes aloud as he shopped in the stores, because it pleased him to say the word "wicking". In fact, he used the word "wick" and its variances as often as he could.

"Excuse me, ma'am, but would you say that this particular shirt wicks away perspiration?"

"I don't know. Does it say anything on the label?"

"Well, let me see. Ah, yes, right here. 'Special fabric that wicks away perspiration.' I suppose that is exactly what I need. In fact, I would like all of my clothes to wick. Would you be so kind as to show me to the wicking section, please? Wick wick wick wick wick."

It cannot be said that our murderer does not find enjoyment in life.

It wasn't two minutes later that Bryony came running up the trail from behind him and whooshed right past his spot in the bushes. Her gait was relaxed and her arms swung loosely as she ran, not that super tight Barbie doll form so many of the women had these days. Women are supposed to look fabulous in a little black dress. They rear the children, are the workplace's brainy sexpot, and cook delicious and nutritious dinners. They write bestselling novels and monitor the house's Internet use while clipping coupons. It was wearing them out. He had noticed that his last few victims gave up on their fight much quicker than the women in the past, and this distressed him. They had a type of weary "Gee, finally-it's-over" sheen that skidded over their eyes like clouds, and it was, to be honest, disappointing. He expected more.

In fact, his last victim gave up so quickly that he grabbed her by the shoulders and shook her.

"Why are you giving up?" he whisper/shouted at her. "This is your life that we're fighting for!"

"I'm tired," she said, and fell limp.

He held the knife up to her throat, and she didn't even flinch. "Your life is so much more precious than you think. You really should have fought for it."

A quick pull of his knife, left to right, and her body

spasmed heavily. He wanted to leave a note on her corpse saying, "She didn't even try to live. The satisfaction I received from this kill was substandard," but he decided against it. For one thing, they might be able to trace the note, and he really didn't want to be caught any time soon. For another . . . it would have been stupid. And Peter Culpert was not a stupid man.

Ah, and now you know his name!

Quickly, quickly, filter it through in your mind and see if you recognize him from anywhere else in the story. Is he from Bryony's hometown? Somebody she works with in the market?

The killer has a name, he has a name. Now that you know, what is the significance of it?

The significance is that he has a name, and it is Peter. That is it. Sometimes when you read too much into a tiny thing, you are bound to be disappointed.

So let us discuss Peter.

Are his crimes completely random? Are they ever deserved? Can they be warded off by good deeds and kindness and talismans and belief?

Peter did not think so. Although his targets were women he didn't know personally, there was always something about them that caught his eye. Perhaps she had particularly sparkly earrings that day, or she reminded him of somebody he knew when he was young. One young woman was listening to Mika, and he, too, listened to Mika occasionally, when he was in a particularly foppish mood, and that was enough to tie them together. And as far as he knew, nothing could ward him off, except for maybe a large dog or aggressive boyfriend, or switch those adjectives, but even those things were temporary distractions.

Women have something sweet and pristine inside of them, a keen desire to be alone and reflect, and sometimes the dog/boyfriend talisman is not wanted.

That is when Peter really has the opportunity to show them what he can do with those wonderful hands of his.

But he didn't consider himself evil, not really. He recognized his hobby wasn't exactly socially acceptable, but that didn't mean anything. There are so many things that aren't socially acceptable these days, but does that make them evil? Of course not! The next person who kindly but misguidedly says: "God bless you!" to a sneezing atheist might get an earful, true, but the "Blesser" would not be labeled as evil, per se. In fact, the very next person that she says: "God bless you!" to might respond with a "Thanks, I am extremely allergic to pollen." and all would be well with the world.

Not that Peter believed that murder and sneezing were exactly the same, of course, but it certainly was an argument that downplayed the horrendous atrocity of his actions, and therefore it was an argument he would very much like to make. Peter nodded resolutely to the blackberry bushes as he thought of this.

Suddenly . . . there was a scream. Not a "woo hoo!" scream or even an "Oh my goodness, I am so very startled! Just you wait until I get home and regale my friends and neighbors with this humorous and/or thrilling tale at parties!" scream. It was a scream of the most heart wrenching kind. It is the scream of a woman who had picked up her skirts and fled from death her entire short life, and suddenly it is staring her right in the face. S realizes even though she thought she was prepared, she isn't, not really. It is the scream of somebody who has so much to live for, so many precious plans, and, in fact, is most certainly going to die.

Chapter Thirty Seven
In Which the Murderer Becomes a Hero

This is what Peter the Murderer thought:

"Wow, what horrible, painful screams. It reminds me of the good old days. That is certainly a woman who wants to survive. Mmm, how lovely."

He thought, "How unusual for somebody else to be on my turf. I certainly don't like it. I just might need to hunt this other person down and have a frank, yet gentlemanly discussion, on what one does and doesn't do when an active serial killer has laid claim to a specific area."

He thought, "The girl."

And once that brief thought ghosted over his mind, he could think no more. "The girl." The girl he hunted, the girl he had gifted, the lonely girl from the stars whose very countenance had been frosted over by death before he even met her, and now?

And now somebody was beating him to her.

That galvanized him. That got his legs moving. He burst out of the blackberry bushes, heedless of the scratches, and pelted down the trail as fast as his legs could take him. Which was plenty fast, because he was a man with a mission.

It took him several seconds to come upon Bryony, who was kicking and screaming as hard as she could, biting at the arm that wrapped itself around her and ducking away from the sharp and distressing knife trying to force her silence.

"Shut up, shut up!" yelled the man who was pulling her off of the trail. He was sweating heavily, obviously perplexed and dismayed at this wisp of a thing who gave him so much more trouble than he anticipated. Droplets of blood speckled the ground, his clothes, ran down Bryony's arms and soaked into her socks and sneakers.

The murderer—the *second* murderer, not our Peter—was making a mess of it. Not a professional, obviously, but more likely a young student at the university who was out for an early morning kill, simply to satiate his curiosity. Or he had done it before, but maybe only once or twice, and he still hadn't developed his skills yet. *Poor guy,* thought Peter. *He really screwed this up. Perhaps he would have had potential, but now nobody will ever know.*

Bryony's wide eyes caught sight of Peter, and she fastened her gaze on him neatly, much like the near perfect sound a snap makes when it clicks together nicely.

"I don't know what to do," her gaze said. "I used every move Rikki-Tikki taught me, which is probably why I'm still alive, but it wasn't enough. It wasn't enough and now I can't seem to get free. Would you be so kind as to offer me your services?"

"Who's Rikki-Tikki?" Peter the Murderer's eyes asked back. "What an unusual sounding name."

"Well, actually, it's Reginald," her eyes explained. "But that's so formal and he doesn't care for it at all. He's just Rikki-Tikki to us, and you'll see what I mean if you ever get to know him. And I'm afraid that might not be very likely, for now this man has seen that you are here, and he's getting even more desperate than he was before, and he's already very shaky with his knife. In fact, I'm suffering quite a lot of pain and fright, and I might very well pass out in a few moments, so please help me as quickly as you can, if you don't mind."

"Oh my goodness," his eyes replied shame-facedly. "Where are my manners? Of course I shall help you. I will just . . . oh dear."

Because, you see, the blood and the fear and the pain and the shock and everything were too much for our Bryony, who simply passed out cold.

This was good for two separate reasons: 1) The young, clumsy killer-in-training wasn't prepared for this, and the weight of her body suddenly going limp threw him off, and 2) Peter the Original Murderer now didn't have any witnesses.

"Why'd you have to choose this one?" he asked the mystified younger killer. "I've been watching her for weeks. You really should have been more careful. There's etiquette, you know."

"I'm . . . sorry?" said the younger killer, but it really didn't matter because it was already too late for him. Peter grabbed the knife from his shaking hand, rammed it into the side of his neck, and watched him bleed out. He dragged the body off the trail and under a particularly camouflaging group of bushes and fallen trees. He had stashed bodies here before, and it did quite nicely in a pinch. He'd sneak back and dispose of the wannabe killer later. Then he returned and sat on the ground, cradling Bryony's head in his lap.

"We'll just wait for somebody to jog by and help us, shall we?" he said. She didn't reply as she was unconscious, and the youthful killer didn't reply either, as he was dead.

Peter sat there in companionable silence with the young woman he knew he would eventually murder, watching her chest move as she breathed, feeling the breath leaving her lungs, and reveling in the fact that they shared the same oxygen, the same *space*. It would be a shame to see her go, really, and for the first time he felt something almost like a stab of regret, but then it was gone. For we are what we are, and he had always thought this, and he was born to be a killer while Bryony was born to be killed, and thus their relationship was set in stone before they ever met. If things had been different, perhaps they would have had a long and healthy friendship, and their children would have played together in the sandbox and on the monkey bars, and they would have gotten together with their respective spouses for neighborly game nights and laughter, but alas, this was never meant to be.

So Peter looked at his ultimate victim, and ran his fingers across the bone under her hair and across her cheek, and down her arms and legs. He was checking the wounds which really were superficial under all the blood. For this he was grateful because he didn't want to wait very long before he killed her, but she needed to be healed first because that was only polite, because that was good form. He wondered what her last words would be and he wished, not for the first time, that somehow he had been able to tell her his name.

"It's Peter," he said to her now. "Peter Culpert."

She didn't answer, and he didn't expect it, and he hummed a sort of calming lullaby as he waited, and plotted exactly where he would twist the knife in her ribs when the time came.

She started to come to, and moved a little.

"Shhhh," he said and stroked her hair. "Everything is going to be all right."

There, he thought, picking out a particularly fine knifing spot. *Right there.*

Chapter Thirty Eight
Sorrow and Stars and Light

Eddie Warshouski was getting tired of Detective Bridger.

"So your old girlfriend and your mother were both murdered, and now your new wife is attacked, as well? You're sort of the Typhoid Mary of killers, aren't you?"

Well, ouch, Eddie thought. *This man pulls no punches.*

"I told you I wasn't in town for my mother's murder. I was getting married. And a man in my girlfriend's building killed her. He was a whack job. And this guy that attacked Bryony—"

He couldn't finish. He was furious. The idea that some sadistic killer would step out on a popular running trail and try to drag his wife off to do who knows what was beyond him. What a horrible and distasteful affair. How absolutely hurtful and unforgivable, whatever he had planned.

Well, he knew what. He knew exactly what this creep had planned to do, and he could hardly think straight. Bryony was still in the hospital, cut and bruised and shaken, but otherwise whole, although they wouldn't let her out for a few more hours as "a precaution".

Eddie wanted to hit something.

This detective, mostly, but it wasn't his fault.

He had spoken with Bryony after she found the body floating in Lake Washington, and he, too, had been unable to deny the tiny bits of her spirit that diamonded out of her eyes and broke upon the floor.

Eddie knew Detective Bridget wanted to protect her because it was his job. Because he was human. Because this was a land of monsters, and right now a monster had gone after a girl made of nothing more than sorrow and stars and light.

Detective Bridger sighed. "Look, Mr. Warshouski, it's my job. I don't like questioning you any more than you like being questioned. I can see in your face you didn't do these things, but I'd be remiss if I didn't ask."

He was not a man to be remiss, Eddie could tell. He sighed, too. "It doesn't seem fair, detective, and that's a funny thing to say because I am not a man who believes life is meant to be fair. But every day we wait. Every time the phone rings, I wonder if it's somebody calling to tell me about Bryony. Every time I see her, I think it is going to be the last time. You don't know how it is, seeing how fragile she can be. Sometimes it is wearying, but I don't regret it. I don't."

He looked at the detective like the man was challenging him, which he wasn't.

"You take care of her," he said seriously. Eddie's eyes flicked up to his, but the detective shook his head emphatically. "I know you are, but something tells me this isn't over yet, that your wife . . . "

"My wife was born to die," Eddie said simply, and

they both sat there for a long time and thought about it, and the words lingered heavily in the air between them, but they rang true. In the other room Peter Culpert was telling another policeman exactly what had happened, how he heard a scream and came running, and chased off the man who tried to take the girl. He was lauded as a hero and a Real Stand Up Guy, and it was an unusual and mildly uncomfortable feeling for Peter. Usually he was laughed at or picked on, and this new feeling was scarier in a way, although not altogether unpleasant. And when Detective Bridger finally told Eddie he could go, Eddie popped into the other room to see the brave and heroic trail runner-turned-white-knight, and invited him to dinner that weekend, to properly thank him for saving his new bride.

The conversation went something like this:

Eddie said, "Hello, I am Eddie and you saved my wife. Her name is Bryony, and she is special and wonderful and very dear to me, and I am afraid without you, she would have been lost. Were you also under the impression that without your intervention she would have been lost?"

Peter said, "Well, she was fighting quite valiantly, so perhaps she would . . . it could have happened that . . . no, she most certainly would have been lost."

Eddie said, "I am ever so grateful to you—" and there was an awkward and expectant pause as Eddie realized that no, he did not know this savior's name, and he was certainly hoping to find out, as it would seem ever so discourteous to call him "Hey you" for the remainder of their lives, especially when he owed this man such a great debt.

Luckily Peter said, "I'm Peter," and they shook hands extremely cordially.

"How do you do?" asked Eddie.

"Very well, thank you," replied Peter.

Eddie said, "Anyway, please come to our home for dinner on Friday night. I'd love for you to see Bryony calm and conscious, and not on hospital drugs. We would really like to thank you properly."

Peter said, "I would be delighted. What a gracious invitation."

To which Eddie replied, "Anytime," and clapped Peter on the back like they were old friends.

Of course they wouldn't be friends at all if Eddie had any idea what Peter was secretly planning, but Eddie is not psychic, and Peter will not come right out and say: "Can't wait to murder your wife in the future. Later, man." So for the moment, at least on the surface, they were friends. And perhaps for that second, their friendship was real, for little is known about Peter and his perception of friendship, and especially male friendship. It could very well be that this moment with Eddie was one of the experiences that he held dearest and closest to his heart. For Peter is a lonely man, a man who constantly surrounds himself with the dead, and this may come as quite a shock to you, dear reader, but the dead are not as friendly and as social as the living. This is true. And a man who reaches out in gratitude, especially a gruff and untouchable man as Eddie, well, it can be hard to resist, and has the tendency to soften even the hardest of hearts.

Yes indeed, Peter was somewhat stunned but also pleased by this unexpected gesture, and he stared at the Warshouski's address in his hands and tried to do some basic calculations.

What he calculated was this: If Eddie goes to see Bryony in the hospital which is seven miles away (with traffic clipping along at a fairly good rate) and he has to kiss every single cut she obtained, and the younger killer had exactly one minute and two seconds to take as many slashes at her tender skin as he could (at a rather paltry rate of one slash every 3.4 seconds), then how long does Peter have to break into their apartment and poke around before Eddie comes back?

What a delightful scenario. Peter always did enjoy math, very much.

Chapter Thirty Nine
Stunning in its Horror

They finally released Bryony from the hospital, and Eddie couldn't help himself: He scooped her up and carried her to the car like an invalid.

"Eddie, I'm all right, I'm all right!" she exclaimed, but she was happy, and kissed Eddie on the cheek, and patted his shoulders, head, and arms with her bandaged hands.

"I invited the man who saved you over for dinner this weekend. His name is Peter Culpert, and he seems nice. I'm happy he was there, Bryony."

"I'm happy, too," she said, and they held hands and climbed the rickety stairs up to Eddie's old apartment, which was now Bryony's new apartment. As soon as they stepped inside Eddie knew something was wrong. His eyes darted around the room as he took everything in.

Jasmine the Guitar was lying two inches farther to the right than he had left her. He knew this because he always lined her up exactly with the vertical stripes on the awful wallpaper. He was a bit obsessive in this way.

The glass in the sink was wrong. Bryony had a

strange habit of flipping every glass that she drank of upside down when she was finished with it. This glass was not flipped upside down.

The door to the bedroom was ajar.

"Bryony, no!" Eddie shouted and reached out to her rather uselessly, as she walked over and flung open the bedroom door. Eddie closed his eyes like a child, as if somehow would protect him from seeing what he knew he would see. A man with a gun waiting for Bryony. A bomb that would suddenly go off, or a guillotine of flashing steel that would zip out of the doorway with a triumphant *hiss Thunk!* Eddie suddenly believed anything was possible in this life. He was paralyzed, waiting for the world to reel.

"Oh, Eddie, it's so beautiful!"

Eddie's eyes flew open and he was across the room and standing beside his wife in a second. Their bed was covered with flowers, hundreds and hundreds of different colored blooms, cascading off the sheets and pooling on the ground like water. It was absolutely stunning in its horror. There were irises and cosmos and tiger lilies and something that looked like Indian Paintbrush, but taller and much finer. There were tulips and daffodils, both yellow and white, and dogwood blooms.

And yes, there were yellow jonquils.

Bryony already had a purple flower in her hair, and when she turned to Eddie, her eyes were radiant.

"Thank you so much! What a magnificent sight, so much life after such a terrible time with that man. The way he looked at me, it made me want . . . I never thought I . . . You're so good to me, my darling."

She walked into his arms and he automatically

closed them around her, and she was bouncing from foot to foot happily, a buzz of exquisite joy, already tossing the terror of this morning aside like discarded clothing, because what was the purpose of it really? Why dwell when there was happiness and life and Eddie and flowers. My word flowers in this very room!

Eddie stared over her head at the spill of blooms, and he wondered how something so friendly and beloved could also be so sinister. He wouldn't have been surprised at all if suddenly they started hissing and rattling their stems in a threatening manner, dragging Bryony into them and filling her mouth and nose with pollen and broken stamens. But no, there they lay, innocent and sweet and full of good feeling. They infused Bryony with a happy pleasure. She was thinking that she was home now, surrounded by flowers the desert could never produce, recently escaped from impending death, and maybe it was over, maybe that was the end of it and she could live, really *live* without always glancing behind her shoulder, and wouldn't that be lovely? Wouldn't that be truly remarkable?

She climbed onto the bed and slipped under the sheets, and the flowers nestled around her, snuggling into her hair and the curves of her body like warm children, and there she fell asleep. It had been such an exhausting day. Eddie pulled up a chair and watched her, unable to bear the idea of touching those flowers. They bared their fangs and snapped at him, but slid their delicate petals soothingly over the gashes on Bryony's white face and arms.

When she dies, she'll look just like this. I will fill her casket with all of the flowers it can hold, and they will love her and she will love them, and she will not be alone.

Except, Eddie had another idea, struggling to break the surface of his misery. The attacks on Bryony seemed to be coming closer together, and although he thought he had understood before, now he realized completely how his life would truly be without her. How dark, how empty of magic. Bryony had swung from the red velvet curtains of mystery that finally opened in his mind, and now that he saw sunlight and tasted pure snow, how was he to live without?

Certainly when the time came, her casket would be full of flowers. But he was beginning to realize now he needed to leave room inside, plenty of room.

Eddie isn't a particularly large man, but he wanted to make sure there was enough room to accommodate him and also Jasmine the Guitar, because he intended to serenade Bryony to sleep every night throughout the eternities.

Chapter Forty
Stitches

"Mr. Culpert, would you mind passing the rolls?"

"Please, call me Peter."

So it was the weekend, and the cozy and sparse apartment was suddenly full of guests. There were Bryony and Eddie, and they had invited Syrina and Rikki-Tikki over, as well, and Peter Culpert—the man who wanted more than anything to murder Bryony—was their guest of honor.

"Thank you so much for saving her life," Syrina said, clasping both of Peter's hands with her own. "I can't imagine what would have happened if you hadn't been there."

Yes, thank goodness I was stalking her from the bushes, Peter thought.

"Yes, thank goodness I was jogging just then," he said aloud. "What a remarkable coincidence."

Rikki-Tikki snorted. "Nah, it wasn't a coincidence. Death sort of has a thing for Bryony, if you know what I mean, and we're all set up like chess players to thwart it sometimes."

Peter tilted his head to the side and looked at

Rikki-Tikki. "Death has a thing for her? Whatever do you mean?"

Bryony studied her hands, now released from the bandages, but still covered with chilling black stitches everywhere. She looked as though she had been sewn together by a mad scientist, and since the doctor was having a particularly bad day when he did the stitches, it wasn't very far from the truth.

Peter looked around the table, and everybody suddenly seemed very interested in their fingers and hands and each other's outfits.

Bryony looked up and smiled. It was painful to see, because her lip was split and her eye was still blackened, but at least most of the cuts on her face were up in her hairline, and the black stitches weren't as noticeable as they could have been. The double rows down the side of her neck, however, were another matter entirely. Syrina's stomach lurched each time she saw them. Rikki-Tikki's face went unnaturally pale. Eddie balled his fists and the muscle in his jaw jumped. Peter shook his head internally and thought: *You were so clumsy, you stupid kid. You really should have practiced before you scarred up a work of art like Bryony. I shall do a much better job of it.*

Conceited? Yes. A bit smug? Certainly. But then Peter Culpert has been killing innocent young women for a long time, and he considers himself to be a master at his work. There is unearned pride, and then there is pride in a job well done, and although his skill is a terrible and atrocious thing, it cannot be said he didn't work long and hard for it. So to be fair, one must give Peter his due, albeit grudgingly.

Hooray, Peter, one cheers halfheartedly. *Such a good job, woo-hoo.*

Now one hopes that the Seattle City Police Department happen to have two or three well-armed officers stumble across Peter in the midst of a murder and they taze him and handcuff him, and put him in a cell for a good long time. Then perhaps the cheering will be a little more exuberant, and the joyous "Yahoos" will ring through the city with unbridled passion and enthusiasm. Wouldn't that be simply splendid!

"It's all right, Peter," Bryony said. "You don't have to talk about it. I'm sure this is quite uncomfortable for you. But we all know, and that is the way of it, and it isn't so big and scary if you just acknowledge it. I am going to die. It has always been this way, and I am used to the fear."

Peter frowned. "I can't believe you just accept your death like that."

When Bryony looked at him, her pale moon eyes showed her sorrow, and our murderer was taken aback. Sorrow? *Sorrow,* in one so vibrant and young?

"And what would you have me do? Would you have me deny it? Pretend that I was going to have a long life full of wonderful things I always hoped for? Oh, how I wish it. It doesn't work like that. I am very happy, in a way. I have no choice but to grab at the things I want, because if I don't, they are going to skitter away. How would that change you, Peter? How would it be, if you knew you didn't have any time, and you had to do the thing you wanted most, right now?"

Peter looked around the table at everybody's faces. They were happy, they were bonded. The house had every vase and extra cup and mug full of excess flowers, and the house was warm, perfumed, full of love and the cold calculations of a killer.

Peter stuffed a roll in his mouth and talked around it.

"Oh, I'd probably do what I wanted most in the world, I guess. There wouldn't be any reason to wait."

Bryony smiled and nodded, but Eddie's eyes were narrowed.

"And what would that be?" he asked Peter. "What do you want more than anything else?"

Peter hesitated and then shrugged. "I don't know. I guess I'd really have to think about it."

That is really the smartest thing he could have possibly done, for what he was thinking was vastly different.

Why Eddie, he thought as he took a mouthful of beef stew, *I would kill your wife. Right here, right now, with everybody watching and helpless in their horror to stop me. That is what I would do.*

"Delicious dinner," he said sincerely, and smiled.

Chapter Forty One
Death Like a Crown

Detective Bridger woke up thrashing.

He gasped and waited for his heart to slow down, which took longer and longer to do.

"Dreaming about that girl again, sweetheart?" asked his wife. Her lovely face was full of sympathy, and traces of apprehension lined her forehead. Her husband had a tender soul and she was beginning to fear for him, because it seemed harder for him to shrug out of the coat of grime and murder he wore home each evening. He was growing distraught and driven and she knew the impending death of this lovely girl was behind it. Although she hadn't seen the woman herself, she believed in her darling Ian, and she believed him when he said this girl wore death like a crown, and the crown was growing heavier and more difficult to endure, and one day her frail bones would snap entirely under the weight of it.

"I have to go over the files again," he said, and then he was gone. She knew he would be locked in the home office for the rest of the night, scouring the files he had gone over a hundred times, searching for something different to give him more insight.

She moved over to his side of the bed and pondered in the darkness. She was frustrated at first, angry and even a little jealous at the attention her husband uncharacteristically lavished on this case.

"What is it about this girl?" she had demanded. She was going to go further and say some particularly unkind things when she saw her husband was searching for the exact words to explain everything to her, so she sat on the bed and listened.

"I spend my whole life finding bodies and then trying to figure out who killed them. It's too late; the damage has already been done but I still try my best so the family can have some peace. Some justice. But this girl . . . " Ian took his wife's hands in his own and spoke earnestly. "If you only saw her, you would know. She is like a small flower blooming from a crack in the busy sidewalk. Beautiful and hopeful, struggling so hard to put down roots somewhere, and it's a delight to see, but at the same time your heart drops and you hold your breath because you know somebody is going to step on that flower and crush it. That is how I see this girl. Her fate is already determined, but she is trying so hard despite that. And her friends! Oh, my darling, you should see how they all fight. It may be the first time I have ever seen real courage. They deserve somebody's help, do you understand that? They've earned it. As for me, this is my chance to find the killer *before* the body is discovered. Perhaps I can stop it before the damage is done. I have to try."

Ian wouldn't be back to bed tonight.

His wife got up and put on some coffee.

Chapter Forty Two
Falling into Fish and Flowers

Eddie no longer spent his days playing Jasmine the Guitar at Pike Place Market.

"Where's your husband?" Chad the Fish Guy asked Bryony one day. He was trying hard not to look at the noticeable stitches on her hands and face, but it was difficult. Bryony helpfully held her hands out for him to inspect. He touched them gingerly.

"He's busy," she said. "He's recording."

Chad the Fish Guy was impressed. "Wow. When things started to take off for him, they really took off." He ran his finger over one of her new scars with some trepidation, but she grinned at him.

"They don't hurt, not really. You don't have to be so gentle. Yes, I'm very happy for Eddie, but I'm sad because I miss him. I'm lonely without him. Are you ever lonely, Chad?"

Chad was always lonely, but he would never say. He was constantly surrounded by people, and especially by women, but he was always lonely. He often curled up in his cold apartment and wished he had somebody warm who would stay with him, or a fun-loving roommate, or a best friend. But that was not to be, at least not for our Chad the Fish Guy, who did not know how to treat women with respect, and didn't know how to treat men besides anything except competition. So, who did he have left? Nobody, that's who.

"I don't get lonely, Bryony," he said jauntily, and Bryony, perhaps sensing those words were big circus balloons full of nothing but popcorn-scented air, stood on her tiptoes and kissed his cheek.

"I am glad we are friends. You are a special man, and special to me, and I want you to know that when the time comes, I am going to have everybody flash through my mind, and when it is your turn, I will take an extra second to reflect on you and think, 'Oh, my favorite fish guy, how I am going to miss him when I am dead.'"

Chad didn't know what to say. He was moved, a new and unusual feeling to him. Usually when he felt any emotion about a woman at all, it was typically desire, and then he would whisk her off to his apartment and promptly become annoyed with her before the evening was through. But he knew that desire was the wrong word for whatever he felt for Bryony. Oh, certainly he entertained little fantasies of her every now and then, especially one where she showed up at the market, knocked Eddie across the head with Jasmine the Guitar, and leapt into Chad's masculine arms crying: "Now that I am free from that awful Eddie, I want you and everybody down here at Pike Place Market to know that Chad Pufferhoff is the man for me. I will use all of my feminine wiles to seduce him into making me Mrs. Pufferhoff, and in the meantime, we shall fall over backward in rapturous joy, landing in either fish or flowers, according to where we are standing at the moment. To wit, to woo!"

But that fantasy and others like it notwithstanding, Chad knew he didn't want to forget Bryony's name one day, and he wouldn't be annoyed with her before the night was over. In fact, he wanted her to be around forever, kind of like the sister he never had. Only he has heard that the words "desire" and "sister" do not go together in the same sentences. So perhaps Bryony isn't quite like a sister to him, but maybe a far off relative, like a second cousin once removed? Chad the Fish Guy Pufferhoff wasn't certain of that either, because Bryony was certainly closer than that. Family relationships are so confusing.

She was looking at him, covered in stitches and shiny new scar tissue, her mouth turned down at the corner because of the cut there. Suddenly Chad was filled with a feeling he had never, ever felt before, and it was all-consuming.

He swept Bryony up into his arms, and her shoes dangled a good two feet off of the ground. "Oh," she said in surprise, and then she was silent, because she knew deep in her heart that Chad had a Very Important Something to say.

"Bryony, you're not my sister or my roommate or even my second cousin once removed, but I have to tell you this: I am jealous of Eddie, he gets to see you stagger around in your bathrobe and I don't. I'm jealous of Syrina who was lucky enough to live with you and I never got that chance. I'm jealous that you have people come over to your house, and I'm not one of them. I want to be your friend. And when you die, I don't know how I'll ever come back to work, because I'll look at your flower stand and there will forever be something missing. Something bright, something that came from the stars. And I've never cared what happened to other people before. You have always been kind to me, and for some reason I want to be kind to you, and it makes the world a different place. I don't know what this feeling is called, but it's not uncomfortable, per se. Just different."

Chad stopped talking and realized he was still holding Bryony. He put her down and stood there awkwardly. Bryony started to laugh.

"Chad, there is a name for that feeling, and it is called love. You love your family and you love your friends. You love me and I love you, and this makes me happy. Perhaps you wouldn't mind keeping an eye on me in the market while Eddie is gone? To make doubly sure I am safe? If it isn't too much to ask."

Chad's chest puffed up with pride, and he was most pleased to help keep watch over perhaps the only friend he would ever know, and he vowed to be vigilant. And this was a kind and gracious thing for him to do, and made him more of a man than anything else in his life. But love, although beautiful, can also be unkind, and one is apt to get his heart broken. This is exactly what happened to our dear friend Chad Pufferhoff turned Fish Guy. For not more than half a week later, Eddie still had not come back to the market, so Chad kept his promised close eye on Bryony, who seemed to be tired and full of sorrow for some reason. And he noticed a man in the background, a man he had seen before two or three times, watching Bryony. Now Chad is a professional at knowing what a man sees in a woman, and he could tell this man wasn't interested in Bryony's smile or her laughter, but was zeroing in on the pulse in her neck, and the short, choppy breaths she occasionally unconsciously took, and something about that made Chad's hackles rise.

This time the man slipped off and headed down into the dark spaces beneath the fish market and Chad wiped his hands and followed him. Down and down they went, farther and farther into the labyrinth. Chad thought he had lost the mysterious man, but turned a blind corner to find that the man waiting.

"So you really were following me," he said conversationally. "Unbelievable."

Chad pulled himself up to his full height, trying to look intimidating. "I think you want to hurt Bryony, and I won't let you do it." His voice was strong, and Chad was proud of himself. *Hmm, loving someone really does give you strength*, he thought. How proud Bryony would be when he told her.

The man didn't look fazed. "Of course I want to hurt her. We're each other's destiny, she and I. I was born to kill, and she was born to die, and isn't that convenient? Lovely, really." Something flashed in his hand, and Chad's mind said "Oh!" and it said "No!" and it tried to say something else, but it was lost in the pain of being stabbed two, three, four times in his chest.

The man sighed. "I was hoping for more. Oh well, thems the breaks." He wiped his knife carefully on Chad's shirt, and stepped smartly away.

Chapter Forty Three
A Broken Heart

This is what Chad thought:

He thought, "Oh, rats, that guy is going to go after Bryony. I have to help her!"

He thought, "Why aren't my legs working? I can't seem to make them move."

He thought, "Just when I figured out how to really love someone . . . "

The sad irony is Chad had finally discovered his heart after many years of denying it. He discovered he loved the girl at the flower shop and, yes, even Eddie for his grouchy protective ways, and with this new knowledge he could have gone on to live a beautiful and productive life.

It could have been a life full of a witty wife and five children and a family dog whose name would have changed bi-weekly due to the whim of the family, although he would have been called 'Buckley" more often than not. Chad could have purchased a home his wife would convince him to paint a whimsical dark purple with white trim, thereby being both creative and tidy, and he would have mowed the lawn every

Saturday morning before a traditional Pufferhoff breakfast with eggs, and pancakes in funny shapes, and milk that always seemed on the edge of expiring, but never quite did.

This life was never to be, however, because this new heart had warned him to watch over his friend, and he had followed its advice for the first time, and what happened?

His heart was, quite literally, ripped apart.

Chapter Forty Four
Meanwhile

While Chad the Fish Guy died alone in a seldom used part of the building, Bryony went to her favorite fruit vendor for their Lunch Special. The Lunch Special cost a dollar fifty and consisted of a freshly plucked peach, a bottle of water, and a paper towel.

"You're looking rather peaked today, my dear," said the kindly old woman who ran the stand. She was picking out the perfect peach, heavy with juice and full of flavor. "You really ought to go home and get some rest."

Bryony accepted the peach and bit into it, careful to keep the juice from running into her rag doll stitches. "This is delicious. Thank you so much. I think I miss Eddie, and I'm tired of . . . everything. I miss my father. I think I might be homesick, but I've never been happier anywhere other than here. Is that not strange?"

Before the old woman could answer, Bryony heard somebody calling her name. She turned to look and there was Peter, his cheeks still flush from his most recent kill, although of course nobody else knew that.

He just looked robust and happy to be in the pleasant Northwest weather.

"What a lovely surprise," he said, and hugged her. "How nice to see you here. Why, really, what are the chances?"

The chances were exceptionally good, considering he had stalked her all the way to work for the past several days, but again, Bryony didn't realize that, nor could she be expected to.

"Oh, Peter! Hello." She introduced him to the vendor. "This is Peter and he's the one who saved me the other day. I'm really grateful to him."

Pleasantries were exchanged ("Oh, you saved her life?" "Why, yes I did!" "Wasn't that sweet of you?" "Why, yes it was!"), and Peter made a show of looking around for Eddie.

"Where's your husband?" he asked.

Bryony's face fell. "He's recording, and then he has a couple of interviews. He's gone quite a bit, lately. And I'm afraid I'm not feeling very well today."

Peter tried not to show his elation, and he did a fine job of it. "Would you like me to take you home, Bryony? You look like you could use some rest."

She agreed and the people at her flower stand let her go half an hour early from her shift. Bryony peered around looking for Chad the Fish Guy, but he was nowhere to be seen.

"I can't find my friend, and I wish I could tell him goodbye. He's almost like a brother to me, and I am going to miss him so much when I . . . I'm being silly, and I'll see him tomorrow." She smiled and took Peter by the hand. "Come on, let's go."

Peter felt her mittened hand in his, and he closed

his eyes for just a second. She was so trusting, making this so easy. It nearly hurt him, and for a second there was a brief stab of conscience, but then it was gone.

"Yes, you'll see him tomorrow," he said as he led her out to his car. "And you'll have a fine reunion."

Chad will be waiting for her with open arms on the other side of this life. Peter the Murderer fingered the knife inside of his pocket.

It was time. It was time.

Chapter Forty Five
In The Murderer's Car

*B*ryony rested her head against the window.

"Peter? I'm . . . I'm not really feeling well. Do you mind if I close my eyes for a little bit?"

Did he mind? Of course he didn't mind, not in the slightest. Wouldn't this be perfect? Wouldn't this be almost romantic in a way, the two of them companionably enclosed in the car, she dreaming sweet dreams and he driving them off somewhere exotic and adventurous?

"Of course I don't mind. You're safe with me." He nearly giggled, but he was not a giggling sort of fellow, so he managed to abstain.

"Can I tell you something?"

He nodded, but realized she couldn't see him with her eyes closed. "Yes," he said aloud, and beamed at how sensitive he could be to her needs.

"When that man was . . . on the trail. When he was . . ."

"When he was trying to kill you," he prompted helpfully. He heard Bryony sigh.

"Yes. When he was trying to kill me, it was strange. I keep seeing his face in my head. I thought I was prepared, you know, because all of my life, I knew. But it felt wrong somehow, like the universe hiccupped and threw everything out of whack. That he stepped out of line and wasn't where he was supposed to be. Like he had somehow interfered in the grand scheme that is my life. Does that make any sense at all?"

Of course it did. The young punk *had* stepped out of line, had crossed another man's boundaries, and it wasn't to be taken lightly.

"It makes sense," he said. He patted her hand reassuringly, pleased that she realized the man who almost murdered her had been the wrong man. How grateful she will be when Peter does it. "Oh, Peter!" she will say, and they will beam at each other happily. "If only I had known that it was you all along! Why, I never would have been afraid! How would you like to go about this? How can I be of the most help to you? Would you like me to close my eyes? Because if that would be better for you, I will most certainly close my eyes. How very wonderfully exciting!"

"Thank you, Peter," she said now. "I felt I could tell you and you would understand. I tried to mention it to Eddie, but . . . anyway, thank you." Her voice was beginning to fade. She was nearly asleep.

They had more in common than she realized, Peter thought.

It was touching in a way, her childlike acceptance. He wished he had more time with her, but he would never get a more perfect opportunity. He would help her upstairs, tuck her into her bed. He would promise to wait with her until Eddie came home, and would sit on the foot of her bed and they would talk, or he would sit in a chair and watch her fall asleep. But no, he wanted her awake for when it happened. He wanted her to remember him, to see his face in her large eyes, to see the color drain away as her throat opens and spills crimson.

Tonight was the night. It was time.

Peter nudged the car along a little faster.

Chapter Forty Six
Priorities

*O*nly *things did* not go as planned for our deviant and murderous Peter. When he pulled up to the Warshouski's apartment, he noticed a car outside. Their car. And when he helped Bryony climb the stairs, they were soon greeted by an agitated Eddie.

"What are you doing home?" Bryony asked happily. Peter echoed the sentiment in his head exactly.

He thought: "Oh no, this was going to be so lovely!"

He thought: "Can I take Eddie out, too?"

He thought: "Not a chance, that is one irate man. Okay, better go!"

He opened his mouth to hand Bryony off to her husband and beat a hasty retreat, but Eddie spoke before he ever had the chance.

"Bryony, it's your father. They called me at the radio station. He had an attack of some kind, and he's not doing well. You need to go home."

Bryony reeled a bit, and Eddie and Peter both reached out to steady her. She steadied herself, however, as she had always done, and she straightened her back.

"All right, Eddie. Can we leave immediately?"

Suddenly Eddie was staring at the ground, and the atmosphere became different somehow. There was a type of tenseness to it, and Bryony titled her head and tried to make her Eddie meet her eyes. He wouldn't.

"Eddie. What aren't you telling me?"

He isn't going to go, thought Peter.

"I . . . can't go," said Eddie.

"What? What do you mean? My father is sick and I have to go, and you're not going to come? What do you have that is so important?"

Eddie looked at the ground. "I have a lot of stuff to do with the station, and recording. I'm doing gigs and interviews all over town, and hopefully I'll start branching out a little. I'm getting my name out there, sweetheart. I'm becoming known."

Bryony looked at Eddie, and if he had looked up at that moment, he would have seen the irises of her eyes bobbing in warm tears, and he would have realized instantly the depth of hurt that she felt. But he worked hard to avoid her eyes and so he missed it. What he heard was her voice, which she fought bravely to keep under control.

"Well, I guess . . . that is important, Eddie. I know how hard you have worked, and I'd hate—" her voice broke a bit, but she quickly cleared her throat and valiantly trooped on. "I'd hate to get in your way. Perhaps Syrina or Rikki-Tikki could come with me."

To protect me from the desert, she thought. *To keep me safe, because I can't go there alone. Not like this. I am sad. I have nothing left inside.*

Eddie studied the flimsy metal railing on the front

porch. It was so fascinating and intricate, and he had never seen it before in such a light.

"I already called them," he said. "Syrina has a performance and Rikki-Tikki is down with a particularly nasty flu. I even thought about Chad, but . . . " He didn't bother to finish the sentence, because the idea of Chad the Fish Guy and Bryony flying anywhere together didn't particularly make him happy.

Especially now that Chad was a rapidly cooling corpse, but neither of them knew that except for Peter, and he certainly wasn't going to say anything about that.

"Eddie," Bryony said. "Please. Please come with me, especially if something is wrong with Daddy. It terrifies me so."

Eddie looked right past Bryony, focusing instead on the trees shivering behind her. As his eyes swept away from her, Bryony felt pieces of her soul break apart and crumble like a worn cliff eventually tumbles into the sea. Eddie wouldn't send her off to her darkest, most bloodthirsty enemy because he was recording, and she knew it. In fact, it was so preposterous. Absurd! There had to be something, or someone, else that made him stay behind. But she couldn't ask, oh, she couldn't ask. What if the weight of his secret was too much? What if he sighed in relief and said, "Bryony, you don't know how wonderful it is to finally tell you. I am being broken under the weight of you. My soul has fallen ill and can't be healed until I am as far from you as possible." After all, hadn't she heard it before?

"I'll go with you. If you want."

That said by Peter, who had ceased wishing himself away and fully brought himself into the conversation. He almost wished he hadn't said it, because oh, the awkwardness. At the same time, there was distress in her voice and he knew he could most likely ease it, and besides, he wanted to see this desert himself. It sounded like a nasty, ancient thing, and if it wanted Bryony dead, then most likely it was going to have her. She was tired and drained, and would be worried about her father, and without Stop and Eddie standing there to guard her, she would most certainly fall. And if the desert took her, Peter the Murderer would be cheated from what he felt was rightfully his. It was as simple as that.

Bryony and Eddie both looked at him. Peter flushed a bit.

"I mean, I'm sorry. I don't mean to intrude, but if you can't go—" He looked at Eddie. "And you're afraid to go alone." He nodded at Bryony. "And your friends can't go, well, maybe I'm better than nothing?"

They both blinked, and to be perfectly honest, Peter's feelings were starting to feel somewhat tender. His presence certainly wasn't that undesirable, was it? He was working hard to present himself as A Good Man, wasn't he? He held doors open for people and dropped his spare change into the hands of the homeless. He never stole the newspaper from his neighbor's yard and he was particularly careful to thank somebody whenever they did something for him. Why, except for the killing people thing, he was about as good as they came. Why couldn't they see that? Were they blind? Had they not grown to care for him at all?

Bryony rubbed her fingers together, the black stitches painfully obvious against her white skin. It angered Peter every time he saw them. Stitches were failure, for if one cut well enough, there would be no reason to stitch, now, would there?

"Would you really be willing to do that, Peter? For me?"

Peter nodded. "Well, sure. I mean, why not, right? That's what friends are for, and stuff." He grinned. "It's kind of like I'm your guardian angel." Then he felt awkward, and shuffled his feet back and forth like he was a fourteen year old at his first school dance.

Life, like puberty, can be wretched.

And then Bryony was in his arms, and she was crying, and Peter patted her back inelegantly and his eyes met Eddie's over her head.

Eddie reached inside the door and grabbed Bryony's suitcase, already packed. He went inside and shut the door gently, leaving Peter to carry the suitcase and guide Bryony down the steps, who was hiccupping and rubbing her eyes like a small girl, dizzied by her disenchantment and her tears. She sobbed all the way to the airport.

Back at their apartment, Eddie stepped into their room and lay down on Bryony's side of the bed. What if this is was the last time he ever saw her? What if she never made it home, and the desert finally knocked her to the ground and sucked the marrow from her bones, and he was *here*? How would that be? How would that be?

Eddie curled on his side and pulled Bryony's pillow

over his head. He wanted the scent of her for as long as he could have it.

Rikki-Tikki had been furious when he heard that Bryony was going alone, and had struggled to get out of bed so he could at least accompany her, but some things weren't meant to be.

"You're being stupid, man. A career isn't worth losing the love of your life. You can always work on your career afterward, you know?"

Afterward. After she was dead. No, he wouldn't be able to forward his career afterward because there would be no afterward, not for him. Not for any of them, really, but especially not for Eddie. But he'd never say this to anybody, it was simply too precious. And anyway, Rikki-Tikki didn't fully understand his situation.

"It's . . . not really the career, Rikki-Tikki. There's something I need to tell you, but don't tell Bryony. It would kill her if she knew. Anyway, I've been doing a lot of work, that's true, but not as much as she thinks. That's not where I've been all of this time."

"I'm not liking the sound of this, Ed."

"You're not going to like it, but I can't take it anymore, I have to tell somebody."

He told Rikki-Tikki, and Rikki-Tikki was silent. Then he asked Eddie to pass a message to Bryony, to tell her something before she left, something Eddie himself had chosen not to say, because the words made him feel sad. It seemed so final. It seemed so hopeless.

The message was this:

It is time.

Run, Star Girl.

Chapter Forty Seven
Bryony Sleeps on Peter's Shoulder

This is what the murderer thought:

He thought, "I can't believe my luck! They're so trusting. Useful."

He thought, "Perhaps she is fated for the desert after all, only . . . with my help."

He thought, "It's not long now."

Beneath the flying airplane, the desert howled and hissed and coiled around itself in painful anticipation. It somehow sensed Bryony's arrival, somehow tasted the soft flesh hidden under her skin. It sucked greedily at what it knew would sate it.

It is time. It is time. The desert always knew it would come.

Chapter Forty Eight
Kill Her

*B*ryony *knew he* wouldn't be there, but she checked the house first.

"Daddy? Daddy?" she called, and ran from room to room.

"Wouldn't he be at the hospital?" Peter asked. It alarmed him to see Bryony worked up to this state, to see her flying wildly around the house like a bird newly thrust into a cage. Where was her serenity? Where was her ethereal acceptance? This panic seemed so unlike her, and it was equally endearing and disconcerting. He silently begged her not to change so that it was like killing an unfamiliar person. He knew exactly how he wanted it to be, what expression he would read in her face and eyes. He wanted to see her hands flutter to the knife and then stop, accepting her fate and his role in it. No, not merely accepting. Embracing. He wanted her to look at his comforting face while her soul finally shrugged off this beautiful yet hindering body, and slipped off to the stars. He didn't want to kill a stranger; he wanted to murder his dear friend.

Peter set the suitcase down and pulled Bryony to

him. It was unusual, hugging a woman who wasn't fighting for her life, and he tried to relax his arms in increments so he didn't harm her. This would take some practice.

"We'll find your dad, Bryony. We'll see him and then you can call Eddie and Syrina and Rikki-Tikki, and tell them that he's fine, that you're fine, that everything is fine. All right?"

She pulled her head back to look at him and the dark circles under her eyes ran down her cheeks until the pale oval of her face was lost in despairing shadow.

"Peter, I love him. I love him and I have missed him terribly while I've been away, and I left him to this desert which is a hateful, horrid thing. I should have come home. I should have run from Eddie and Syrina and everybody else long ago, and now it's too late. I have friends, and a husband, and people that I look forward to seeing at the flower shop. They are in danger, and my father worries about me. I stayed too long, and now I have ruined everything for so many people."

His bird, his Star Girl, was splitting apart. He held the flesh of one in his arms but the other was flitting around, unable to be calmed, incapable of landing. Her clawed feet kept catching at his hair as she ricocheted from wall to wall, ceiling to floor.

"Bryony, we'll find him."

"It's too late, it's too late. What have I done?"

"I said we'll find him."

The desert crackled with laughter.

Peter's head ached, his back hurt, his arms were tightening of their own accord around the fragile skeleton running beneath Bryony's skin, it would soon be powder, it would soon be dust, and everything would end. She'd scatter to the wind and the desert would open its mouth eagerly, catching her on its tongue, and it would be satiated.

Bryony's breath had gone shallow. Her eyes were wide and unseeing. Peter abruptly released her.

"Oh, Bryony, I'm so sorry. It's this house, this land outside of it. It's telling me to kill you, to feed you to it, and I've never had anything quite like this happen before. I'm not myself, it's not letting me be myself, and I'm not a tool for it to use. I refuse." He closed his eyes, took a deep breath. The Bryony birds formed one complete Bryony again, and her gray eyes were focused on Peter's white face. He tried again, quieting all of the voices and the screaming of the desert.

"Let's find your father. Then let's get out of here."

She nodded, once, and was out the door without another word.

Peter was shaking, he had to admit it. And he was furious. How dare this land of sand and bones call to him like that, bow him down to it? He would not. He would not. Bryony was his kill and his kill alone, and the desert would simply go without. That's the way that it was. That was the way he would make it be.

Peter ducked out of the door after her.

Chapter Forty Nine
Stop

Stop was indeed in the town's tiny hospital, which was little more than a glorified clinic, really. They delivered babies there and bound up broken bones and put Branny Jacob's eye back in after Tom Kidd had popped it out with the butt of his knife, though. Twice. "The first time you pop out my eye, shame on you," the nurse said to Branny after he came to, "but the second time that you do it, shame on me

Stop lay in bed, hooked up to tubes and monitors and wires. His hospital gown was on backward so they could easily reach in and adjust all manner of medical doodads on his chest, and he had an IV slowly dripping a clear, benign looking substance from a bag into a long tube that ended on the back of his hand.

"Oh, Daddy," Bryony said, dropping to her knees beside the bed. She kissed her father's shriveled hands and smoothed his white hair away from his gray face. "I have missed you so much, and talking to you on the phone isn't enough. I need to see you with my own eyes and feel you with my own fingers, and you need to do the same. We're alive, Daddy. We're alive."

Stop smiled at her wanly, and then his eyes traveled up to the man who stood in the doorway. His smile quickly became a frown, and Bryony wished she had not seen it: a tired trace of a smile that slipped and fell farther and farther until it was a rainbow of ill feeling.

"Who is this?" he asked. "Where is Eddie?"

Peter tried to look strong and helpful, but the old man's expression didn't change when his daughter explained.

"This is Peter. He's the man who saved my life on the trail. Eddie couldn't come. Things are going very well for him with his music, and he simply couldn't . . . he wasn't able to come, Daddy. But I'm here, and Peter came to make sure of my safety."

Stop's expression darkened as he eyed Peter, and Bryony said brightly, "So how are you feeling now? You certainly gave me a scare. What did the doctor say?"

Stop sighed. "The doctor says it's a heart attack, brought on by stress, most likely. Says he."

Bryony, being the type of daughter she is, read her father very well. "But you think it's something different. What is it?"

Stop looked her dead in the eyes. "It's the desert, honey. It is time, and it is coming for you, and it doesn't want me around to stop it. I am an old man but I still have power, and the desert is sweeping me away." His eyes flicked back at Peter. "He shouldn't be here, sweetheart. Eddie should."

"Daddy, I told you that Eddie—"

Stop wrapped his frail fingers carefully around hers. "Honey. My heart is going to stop now. I can feel it slowing down, and it is my time to go. I am sorry to leave you, but I don't want you to be sad. It's hard, sweetie," he said, as tears coursed down her face, "and I know that it is going to hurt you badly for a while. But know this: I love you, and I am very proud of you, and you have made me happy. I want you to live. I want you to live, my darling girl, and to do so, you need to run. Leave this place, for the desert speaks to me at night and it craves your bones in a monstrous way. The things it tells me at night, the things that it says . . . they are horrible. This is what has damaged my heart. It chips away each time the desert vomits out its plans for you. Now listen to me carefully: You must leave this man. Immediately. Tonight, honey."

"But Daddy, he saved me. He has been watching over me and protecting me."

Stop's eyes were losing their sparkle. They were losing their luster. This distressed Bryony more than she could possibly express, but she wanted her father to remember her as a happy girl who was admirably pulled together, not as a weeping child-woman who threw herself onto his bed and begged him not to go, which was what she really wanted to do. He was both her father and her mother, he was the one that always loved her and cared for her, and taught her how to read and write and listen to the desert. He was strength, even in his physical frailty, and with Stop gone, she was going to be lost, she just knew it.

Daddy, she thought, *don't go. Don't leave me. I can't do this without you, and I have been so tired lately, and something is wrong with Eddie, and I am so scared to be here right now. Don't let the desert win. Don't let it take you! I want to be your little girl*

*forever, and know you will always love me, and won't
turn away from what I have to do. Please, Daddy.*

But she is a kind girl, our dear Bryony, and she kept
these thoughts to herself, never to be heard by anyone
else. Instead she chose to say, "I love you, Daddy. Don't
worry about me. I will be very careful."

Stop's gaze floated from Bryony to the man in the
doorframe.

"You can't have her," he said with what strength he
had left. "You can't have my little girl. I know what you
are, and I say she isn't meant for you."

"Daddy," Bryony said, but the blipping machine
ceased to blip and a distressing flat *beeeeeeeep* ran.
Bryony's tears flowed again in earnest. The quiet room
suddenly became a place of pounding feet and harried
nurses, and Bryony couldn't move, but continued to
kneel there and weep over the corpse of her father.

Peter stepped forward and rested a hand on her
shoulder. "I'm sorry, Bryony. I really am."

She accepted his hand, but her heart shred itself
into tinier and tinier pieces. Her father's last words
hadn't been for her but for this stranger, and his eyes
had been seeing him and him alone. This hurt Bryony,
and made her jealous, which made her feel
unreasonable, and then repentant, and then she
thought of her father. She felt something strong and
good inside of her turn its face to the wall and die.

"I think that my h-heart is b-breaking," she said,
and thought she had never cried so much, not in such
a short amount of time, and it wearied her. Where was
Eddie? Where was her husband? Why was she alone
with the desert and Stop's cooling body and this
strange man that looked at her with a light in his eyes

she now found disconcerting? Why was she alone? Why was she alone?

"You're not alone," Peter said, as though he could hear her. "I am with you. I am always with you. Come, Bryony, let's go back to the house. Let them take care of your father, and I'll take care of you. Let me take care of you."

She was a zombie, she was undead. She was what she had always been, and that was thinly tethered to this world by a silken cord, and it was starting to unravel. Tonight. Tonight.

"Tonight is the night," she whispered. "Tonight is when it all happens."

"What was that, dear?" Peter asked in his most comforting voice. He had been practicing it under his breath, and it came out in a rather satisfactory manner. He was quite pleased with himself. He helped Bryony to her feet and put his arm around her, guiding her toward the door. Toward the desert, and away from her father.

She isn't meant for you, her father said. His final words, and they were so full of his stalwartness and protectiveness and the fire he always stoked in his warm, warm heart. *She isn't meant for you,* said to the man that now had his arms around her. This was wrong, he shouldn't be here. It should be Eddie or Syrina or Rikki-Tikki or even Chad the Fish Guy, but not this man, this man who pulled her out of the arms of a killer on the trail, but had been covered in blood himself. Bryony had woken up to Peter's ethereal smiling face splashed with crimson. Her blood, sure, although more than once she wondered if it was truly all hers, or if some of it had belonged to her would-be murderer. There was so much and they had never found the other man after Peter chased him off...but how could she think such a thing when Peter had been so kind as to help her then, as he was helping her now?

Oh, how Bryony's head spun.

Her thoughts were tumbling like chips of plastic in a kaleidoscope, and she told herself it was merely shock, and the loss of . . . the death of . . . losing her father, her father.

"Daddy," she said aloud, and began to cry again, so hard she could scarcely walk, she clung to Peter's sleeve with her girlish fingers, being guided as though she were blind. Finally he picked her up and carried her out to the car.

Somebody was walking down the street right then, and stood on the sidewalk and watched silently. It was Teddy Baker, Bryony's first kiss, and he stood very still as he watched the stranger situate Bryony in the car and safely belt her in. He nodded politely to Teddy, and Teddy nodded politely back, and the man got into the driver's seat and drove away.

Teddy tucked his hands into his pockets and watched until the car disappeared on the flat, dusty road.

Chapter Fifty
Teddy Baker

This is what Teddy Baker thought:

He thought, "I recognize the look in that man's eyes. It shone from my own eyes long ago. He is going to kill Bryony, and she seems too weak to notice. That is not like her. Something is wrong."

He thought, "Why is she with him and not with her husband?"

He thought, "Am I willing to risk my life to save hers again? It really is her fate to die, it has always been so, and who am I to deny it?"

His heart, which had been stretched by his wife, and even more by his baby girl, was big enough to encompass the Star Girl. Besides, he still recalled their one and only kiss, and how it felt, and the sweet sound of her breathing as she leaned toward him, and his certainty that she would not be breathing in the morning if he got his way. That kiss, her breathing, and her guileless gray eyes had made his heart chant the same mantra it was chanting now.

Something is wrong. Something is wrong. Something is wrong.

And human nature seldom changes. The type of person you are as a child still manifests itself in the way you conduct yourself as an adult, and Teddy Baker was certainly no different. When he was young and faced with the decision of What To Do With Bryony, he decided to save her. Let her live, let her be free. It was only right then, and it was only right now, and somewhere deep inside of Teddy, his younger self rose and stretched and looked out at the world with unexpectedly fierce eyes, and nodded his head resolutely.

Chapter Fifty One
Sorrow

"I'm sorry, but I have to be alone for a while," Bryony said to Peter. He nodded and stepped outside, quietly closing the screen door behind him. Bryony wandered around her childhood home, touching the walls and running her hands over the counters, shiny from years of use. She picked up the phone, called Eddie, and let it ring and ring and ring.

"Hey, it's Eddie. Leave a message, will ya?"

There was a beep, and Bryony didn't know what to say for a long time. She wanted to be positive; she wanted to make sure he didn't worry. He had so much to concentrate on, after all. But at the same time, she wanted him to realize how hurt she was. She wanted him to be on his knees saying: "Baby, I'm so sorry, please forgive me. How could I ever have been so misguided?" They would then fling themselves at each other and there would be tears and warm kisses and they'd rub the tips of their noses cozily together.

Now all was *not* well, and this very real not-wellness made it hard for Bryony to say what she wanted to say. "How dare you? How could you leave me? Don't you know I need you more than I have ever needed anyone? Don't you know I have never been so weak, never been so fragile, and you aren't here? How could you send another man to look after me, when I wear the ring that binds me to you, when I love you, when you swore you'd treasure me until the time came?"

Eddie's phone clicked off. She had waited too long. Still she held the receiver to her ear, and thought, and finally whispered to the dead air what she should have said to his answering machine.

"I love you, Eddie. We lost a baby when I was attacked, and I didn't know how to tell you. I wanted to name her after your mother, or even possibly after mine, but it's too late. It's always too late. I almost wish I had died that day, that I wasn't tortured by being forced to go on without her, and now without you.

"Goodbye, my love."

The phone slid gently into the cradle with the sound of something that knows where it belongs. It belongs in the cradle as Bryony belongs with Eddie, and as their child had belonged to both of them. It didn't seem fair, and with an uncharacteristic surge of anger, she knocked the phone out of its cradle until it lay on the floor, showing its belly in shock and confusion and a terrible vulnerability, making a lonely beeping call that said, "I am loose, I am unbound. I am not where I am supposed to be. Help me, please help me. Put me back because I am quite incapable of doing it by myself."

It was a heart wrenching sound, and yet Bryony couldn't make herself slide the receiver into its cradle, for she feared the final, smug click. Much easier for her to back away, and then finally turn and run for another part of the house, somewhere safer and kinder and much more sensitive to her thoughts and feelings. Somewhere that would try its best to remind her of her childhood instead of how things had gone terribly wrong, and how she had been abandoned by her child and father and husband.

So who was left? Who was left?

Peter was left. And yet . . . and yet that thought wasn't comforting, not in the least, and merely thinking of his name gave her the sad feeling she felt when she watched the stars fall. Bryony fled to her room, and crawled under the covers, and cried like a woman who had tried so hard, and given so much, and had her love and life taken away piece by piece by piece.

Chapter Fifty Two
Rescue

There was a tapping on Bryony's bedroom window. She awoke slowly, groggy and disoriented. The thoughts of her father, Eddie, and her sweet unborn baby slammed into her, and she wearily realized this was life. It wasn't going to get much better. She had been programmed to flee for the promise and hope of a better world, when perhaps the best thing to do would be turn over and close her eyes so she wouldn't see the face of death when it overtook her.

Then more tapping.

Bryony slipped out of bed, opened the window, and peered out onto the street. There stood Teddy Baker, half hidden behind the rough dry brush in the yard.

Why, it was her girlhood fantasy come true. How very bizarre.

"Teddy, what are you doing here?"

Teddy smiled at her. "Nobody calls me Teddy anymore. I've gone by Ted for the last ten years."

"Oh, I'm sorry, I didn't—"

"No, don't apologize, Bryony. I like it. It reminds me . . . of a time long ago, and I realize now that is a good thing to remember." The smile dropped off of his face. "I need to tell you something, and it is extremely important. I know you're in a state because of your father. Are you alert enough to understand what I'm saying?"

Ah, dear Teddy. So concerned and trying terribly to do the right thing.

"Yes," Bryony said. "Please go on."

"Well," he said, and it looked as though perhaps he was blushing, although one could never be sure under the moon, but it is popular opinion that yes, indeed, he was blushing rather madly as he said this. "I have come to rescue you."

There was silence for a long while.

"Do I . . . particularly need saving at the moment? I mean, more than usual?"

Teddy sighed. "You do. My wife and I discussed it. The second she saw you at your wedding, she turned to me and said: 'That young woman is going to die.' And I said: 'Yes. It won't be long now, I think.' And she said: 'If you ever get the chance, you have to save her. Promise me.' I'd promise her anything. So when I saw you with that guy—"

"Peter."

"What?"

"His name is Peter."

"Okay. So when I saw you with that guy, I knew you needed me. Because you don't seem to realize what he has inside him, what has taken up residence inside of his head and pushes its face to his eyes so it can see. His eyes, they truly are windows, and when I look into them, I see what is looking out at me. It is plain to see, but you seem so unaware."

"What do you mean?"

"Exactly," Teddy said. "So I told my wife I was going to come over here and tell you to get out. To leave. It's not safe for you, Bryony, and I don't think you know who that guy is."

"He's Peter."

Teddy took a deep breath. "I don't think you know *what* that guy is, then. He's a killer. I saw it in his eyes; I saw it in the way he looked at you. I know that look, Bryony, and he's going to be the end of you. You have to leave this place."

"But my father—"

"Stop wanted you to live. More than anything else, right? More than anything else, Bryony."

Bryony ran her hand through her hair. The stars on her bracelet shone in the moonlight.

"I will bury him for you," Teddy said gently. "I know you wanted to be here, but if you stay, you will not survive. What about your husband? If you stay, you will never see him again."

Eddie. He had disappointed her, surely, but had she not disappointed him in the past? She hoped they would have the opportunity to disappoint each other in the future. She had to get back to her husband.

Teddy reached into the backpack at his feet.

"Here," he said, and tossed Bryony a pair of white running shoes.

"What are these for?" she asked him, holding them in her hands. She looked at Teddy, who shrugged a bit, as if he too were baffled. The shoes were worn and sturdy and somehow felt like salvation.

"My wife told me to bring them to you tonight. She figured you didn't have time to think about what to pack, that you just hopped on a plane. They're hers. She said you would need them. You have to leave this place. Can't you hear the desert screaming for you? It has gone mad. It's time."

It's time. It's time. It sounded like her father's voice in the wind.

Run, Star Girl.

Chapter Fifty Three
Please Live

*B*ryony nodded, and clutched the shoes to her chest like a talisman.

"Thank you so much, Teddy. It can't be easy to come here and say this to me. In my heart I think I always knew Peter was what you say, but I don't want to believe that, you see. It means I have been foolish, which I have, and that Eddie has been blind, which he has. It means I should have run a long time ago, and I didn't, and now I am sorry. It means when he saved me, he didn't do it because he's a good person, and I so dearly want him to be a good person. Please thank your wife for me, and kiss your beautiful girl, and take care of my father for me. Place him in the desert, and let him tamp it down and hold it back. I fear I shall never return here. Never again. I have nothing to come back for."

Teddy leaned through the window, kissed Bryony on her cheek and ran his hand over the stitches on her face.

"I wish I could help more than this, but I can't. Please live, sweet girl. You give all of us so much hope."

He smiled, and then he was gone, and there was nothing outside except for the sound of the sand shifting and blowing over the rock.

Bryony studied the shoes and realized she hadn't gone running since the day she was attacked and very nearly killed. She slipped them onto her feet and tied the laces, remembering when she and Stop worked on tying her shoes every night.

"It's important to tie your shoes," her father had told her. "Tie them well and you can keep your shoes on your feet. You don't want them to slip off when you are walking or climbing trees or skipping rope. You don't want them to fall off when you run." The words were Heavy With Meaning, but Bryony was only five and didn't understand words Heavy With Meaning, but she did understand things that were important to a little girl.

"And my teacher will be so proud of me!" Bryony said.

"And your teacher will be so proud of you," Stop agreed.

Now she looked around her bedroom one last time. It was full of color and whimsy and bells and chimes and wonderful flying things that hung from the ceiling. There were stars. Stars on the walls and stars on her dresser. Notebooks with stars and plastic stars and stars made out of crystal. It was a beautiful place, and many happy years were spent here, but it had come to an end. It was too dangerous, and she had skirted the issue too long, and her luck was running out, if it hadn't already done so.

"Bye, Daddy," she whispered. "I love you. I'm going to do my best."

Then she slipped out of the window, landing as quietly as she could in the sand outside. She ran quickly to the car, grateful that it was still the same old small town where everybody simply left their keys in the ignition, and hopped inside.

She was going home.

Chapter Fifty Four
Ideally

*P*eter woke up with a start. Something was wrong. What was it? What was it?

He was somewhere unfamiliar, and this realization had him on his feet beside the bed in no time. Had he been caught? Had he been taken? He would rather die before being taken, and he didn't remember a struggle of any sort whatsoever.

A quick scan of the room jogged his memory. Ah, yes. This was Stop's house, the home where Bryony grew up, and he was sleeping in the bed of a dead man, but being who he was meant this didn't bother him any. Stop had seemed like a good and decent man, and heaven knows his daughter adored him, and the fact that he had disliked Peter on sight, well, it only said good things about him, too.

Downstairs Bryony would be sleeping, curled up on her side with, he imagined, her fingers close to her mouth like a child. She had fallen asleep in her clothes, but if she had the time to choose whatever she wanted to wear, would she be wearing a white nightgown to complete the look of innocence? Would she be sleeping in one of Eddie's shirts because she missed him? Her father died and that man couldn't even make the effort to be here. He was undeserving, especially when he knew the consequences of being lax. And there would definitely be consequences. Perhaps after Bryony's death, Peter should finish off Eddie, who would no doubt be grateful for it. Although, actually, Peter most likely wouldn't get the chance, since he could see in Eddie's posture he was trying to make himself smaller and smaller so the world wouldn't miss him so much when he took his own life after his bride's death. Ah, Eddie, so sweet and so misguided. *Hang around for a while,* Peter thought. *Let me do the deed for you. It will give us all what we want.*

Peter stood there musing, and suddenly his eyes darted to the side in reflex. There it was, the sound, the sick, grating sound that woke him. It was the sound of an engine trying to turn over, and as he recognized it, a grim smile crept onto his lips, cementing itself to his face in defiance. After checking on the exhausted woman in bed, holding her hand and stroking her hair while she slept, Peter tinkered with the car just enough that it wouldn't be able to start.

Why would he do such a thing, one would suppose?

Peter is a predator, and a predator needs his prey in order to fully feel complete. If said prey is intent on slipping off and dying alone in the middle of nowhere, well, it leaves the predator with nothing to show for his concentrated effort. Peter had spent a considerable amount of time on this—his perfect kill.

Why else had he taken the time to know Bryony and her friends and even her grouchy husband, for crying out loud.

He had killed those close to her. He had insinuated himself into her life discreetly, in such a way she would be certain to miss him at least a little if he ever decided to slip out of it.

That might be the greatest triumph of all.

Would she weep if she never saw him again? Good thing they'll never have to find out.

He walked to the window and peered outside. He could see Byrony's pale hair in the driver's side window. Apparently it was time.

Ideally, he would have liked her stitches to have been removed. He would have liked her grief to fall from her body like a silk robe. She should have been healthy and happy. He wanted to bleed her innocence from her. He wanted to watch the levels of her joy run out of her veins and they could have smiled at it together, her head on his shoulder as they calmly watched the blood flow. "You have released me from this parasol of horror that has always followed me. I could never truly rest, but thanks to you, Peter Culpert, I shall finally experience true peace. I am ever so grateful."

"You are very welcome," he would answer back genteelly. "I have never had the pleasure of killing a victim as fine as you. It is a joy."

"I wish you many more victims," she would say. Her voice fading, but she would continue to be her polite and caring self until her last breath.

Our brave, brave Bryony! Her hand would slip and fall to the ground, and the blood would be a beautiful pool of life, and their hearts would swim in it like quietly delighted fish.

Peter would kiss her on her unearthly white brow.

"Goodbye, my girl. From the stars you came and to the stars you will go," he would say, and—

No, that sounded too scripted. Perhaps this:

"Goodbye, my girl. Return to your rightful place in the stars, where you will watch over all of mankind throughout the eternities—"

Ugh, that was even worse. Peter leaned his head against the coolness of the window and closed his eyes. Nothing so grand it seemed unbelievable.

"Goodbye, young woman. I hope that—"

Not a chance.

"Your time on earth was short, yet in that brief time you managed to touch many lives."

Yech! Peter's eyebrows furrowed. He wanted to say something meaningful, even profound, but he didn't want the last thing she heard to be a formal eulogy. Or did it sound more like something from a fortune cookie? What to say, what to say.

He had it.

As Bryony's hand slipped to the ground, he would pick it up and gently kiss her fingers.

"Goodbye, Star Girl," he would say.

Perfect. Perfect. That is exactly what he is going to say.

He opened his eyes and looked for Bryony. The driver side door was open, and she was nowhere to be seen.

Peter cursed and reached for his knife.

Obviously this situation was going to be less than ideal.

Chapter Fifty Five
Clouds

The car wouldn't start, and Bryony knew this was unusual. Didn't it start perfectly only today? Hadn't it been a good and serviceable vehicle? Now, suddenly when she needed it most, it chose to let its internal parts rust and die and spew fluid hither and yon?

She didn't think so.

Bryony peeked up and saw a man in the window of her father's room. At first her heart skidded to a stop—Daddy!—but then she remembered her father was dead, and the man silhouetted there was Peter, and she had been warned against him within the last few hours by two people who cared for her.

And she was a kind girl, a tender girl, but she was also a smart girl when her eyes were opened, and her father and Teddy succeeded in opening her eyes. Peter didn't move from the window, and his body language told Bryony he was most likely off in a world of his own, so she used this to her advantage. She opened the car door as quietly as she could, slid out, and hit the ground doing what she did best.

The wind tore through her hair and left a confused

wake behind her. Her feet pounded against the hardened desert sand, and her lungs prepared themselves for the effort they would soon be feeling.

She was alive. She was alive.

Bryony had never run through the desert before. It was too hungry, too eager to trip her up and throw itself on top of her in a flurry of dunes. This was freedom, though, this was joy. She ran from the house, hoping to make it to the edge of town where she would hide in the old library until she could figure out what to do. Call Eddie, most likely. Call Syrina and Rikki-Tikki. Call a cab, call a priest, call for Simply-Tim-The-Police-Officer-Soon-To-Be-President, call for her father, whatever she needed to do.

The ground trembled beneath her, but she caught her stride. It was an easy, loping run. She paced herself, giving herself enough energy to sprint at the end if she needed to. She was afraid that she would need to, that somehow there would be a tornado or some other piece of desert related insanity that would come after her. There is an ancient evil out there, and when it wants you, it wants you. She knew this, and ran evenly. Breathing in, breathing out, trying not to cough on the dust dancing through the air, and woo-hooed its way down the rollercoaster of her throat and into her lungs.

She could do this. She would do this. She was her daddy's girl.

Clouds gathered above her and the air grew dense with moisture. Thunder rolled in the background, and Bryony remembered riding on her father's shoulders as a girl. She held an umbrella over both of them, and

Stop splashed through the puddles with the boundless energy of a young man trying his hardest to keep his daughter from missing her absent mother.

"The thunder scares me, Daddy," she had said.

"The thunder isn't what you have to worry about, honey. It's the lightning, and sometimes even the rain."

"Why the rain?"

"Well," he said, "out here the rain doesn't get to come very often. So when it does, it's angry, and feels like it wants to get back at you for not letting it come. It falls on your head and your hands and your arms, and it hurts. It feels like something hard is being thrown at you. That's not all. It is angry at the desert, and it beats at it with its fists. The desert isn't used to being challenged, you know, and for a while it is overwhelmed. It doesn't know how to fight back against this horrible, hateful rain, and it floods. When that happens—"

"Yes, Daddy?"

"When that happens, all of the desert animals have nowhere to go. They get washed away in the mud and the rain, and all they want is to be somewhere safe. That makes sense, doesn't it, my girl?"

"Of course, Daddy. Can't they just go home to be safe?"

"No, sweetheart. The rain has made everything wet and unwelcome and cold and unfriendly. Their homes are no longer safe. But in the distance, they see something strong and tall that isn't bowed down by the rain, so they all head straight for that."

"And what is this tall and strong thing, Daddy?"

"Oh, Bryony. It's us. Don't be caught in the desert

rain, because all of the terrified, furious animals will head straight for you."

That was many years ago, but Bryony remembered it clearly as her muscles stretched and worked. She had a good five miles to go, and she could make it that far if she was careful, but she was tired, and scared, and most of all, she was lonely.

Eddie, why didn't you come? she thought. *Why aren't you here? I fear we have made a terrible mistake, you and I. I fear it might be our last one together. Oh, how I would love to make more mistakes with you.*

There was a growl of thunder, and there was no masking its anger. The earth rolled under her feet, once, twice. She nearly tripped, but caught herself and continued on. She wished the houses were closer together, but it's not the way it was, for this town had been planned for people with herds of animals and coops of chickens and whatever it is that one calls a group of peacocks. These animals need lots and lots of room, and the homes were spread quite far apart on the dusty, bumpy stretch of desert sand they called the Main Road. Besides, Bryony learned early on it isn't worthwhile to wish for things that would never be.

She looked up at the clouds. How sinister, how unkind. How dark and hateful they seemed to be.

"Why?" she wanted to ask them. "Why do you loathe me so much, when I have always enjoyed watching you roll across the sky? I always found shapes in you, and chose to see the most beautiful things I could so you would be happy. Why can't you just love me in return?"

The clouds didn't answer, being the aloof, scattered

things they are. They are wistful and wishful and really don't care much about the concerns of those who prattle on beneath them. They are very different from stars, which are quite concerned with the antics of earth. Stars choose you, and watch over you, and are interested in what you say and to whom you say it. They are inquisitive. They are compassionate. They would most certainly come to the aid of the Star Girl if they could, for she certainly is one of their own born to the flesh.

"Yes, yes, let us help you!" they chimed, for it is well known that stars do not twitter as much as chime like small bells. "We long for your life! We want to continue to watch you and Eddie and your friends, and see what people give to your children for their birthday, and we want to know which lucky animal will be your first pet and we want you to grow flowers. Lots and lots of flowers. Do not be afraid, Bryony. We are with you, forever and ever, and although we may be weak, there are many of us, and if we all gather together—"

The stars were hushed even in the midst of their exultant cries, for the clouds, you see, had grown weary of them, and rolled in ominously. They linked their arms together and formed a barrier against the stars, and with all of the lights of heaven effectively shut out everything became horribly, horribly dark. Bryony's heart cried out in what might have been, and in fact was, despair.

"No," she thought. "No!" And her footsteps faltered for just a moment before she forcibly pulled herself together and ran on. But in that brief second of silence where she was afraid and unsure, she heard something. It was a second set of footsteps, fast and fleeing through the night, and they were coming from her home, and they were right behind her.

Chapter Fifty Six
The Knife

The thing that must be remembered about Peter is that he, too, is a runner. Whereas Bryony planned to keep a little extra energy in her tank so as to make it the entire five miles, Peter had no such plans. He was sprinting, because he did not need to make it to the edge of town: he only needed to make it to the girl.

His feet hit the ground like pistons, cold and mechanical, and he held the knife tightly in his grip, blade down.

Oh, oh, how tragically this shall unfold.

Chapter Fifty Seven
The Chase

The first drop of rain hit Bryony beside her eye, and ran down her face like tears.

No, she thought. *No!*

She knew Peter was behind her, and her mind went cottony with despair and panic. More time! She needed more time.

Bryony picked up her pace. It would deplete her energy faster, but if she didn't outrun him, her reserve of energy certainly wouldn't do her any good.

She scrapped her earlier plan of hiding in the library and phoning for help. Plan B consisted of running to the closest house and screaming hysterically for help. Unfortunately for her, that was still a good four miles. Loneliness consumed her, biting at her cheeks like the stormy air. It was all catching up with her. It was catching up.

It *was* catching up. Already Peter could see her pale hair gathering and reflecting the weak light that somehow managed to filter through the harsh clouds. She was glowing, an ethereal will-o-wisp, and thoughts of the old tales flitted through his mind. If he followed her, what would he find? Treasure? Tragedy? Ooh, he was hoping for tragedy.

"Bryony, why are you running?" he called. He hoped he had the right note of concern in his voice. "I'm worried about you! Wait for me!"

She didn't stop, didn't even slow. If anything, she kicked it up a notch and ran faster. *Well, so much for that tactic,* Peter thought, and really it was quite a relief to him. Pretending to be thinking one thing when actually he was thinking another was far more difficult than one would imagine. What a relief to be who he really was.

Now he was able to fully enjoy the chase.

Bryony was not enjoying the chase. She was terrified. Her muscles were starting to hurt, stiff from lack of use and proper stretching. Her bruised ribs ached; her eye was still tender even though the blackness was fading. She was breaking down. She was broken.

Something happened then. Either she tripped over something half buried in the sand, or it rose up malevolently in the dark to catch her foot. She went flying, landing hard on the ground. Her body screamed out, and she felt stitches burst. The desert threw a net of desolation around her, and nearly caught her fast, but Bryony was on her knees, crawling. Then she was on her feet. Although limping, she started to gain speed again. She set off, ignoring the water falling from the sky, chilling her. She could almost taste her freedom except

for the hand

reaching from behind

and wrapping itself in her hair.

Chapter Fifty Eight
Fight

*B*ryony," *Peter huffed.* "I wish you were feeling better, that you were whole. You have no idea how much I wish this for you. Alas, it is not meant to be, because it is time. You and I have a dance to finish, don't we?"

The wind picked up, blowing the storm their way, blowing Bryony's hair around her white face like a flag signaling for help. But no help was to be had, and she was stuck fast while Peter pressed behind her, his hand fisted in her hair.

Bryony's head was pulled sharply back, and the wind caressed her vulnerable throat in a way that unnerved her.

She tried to keep her voice calm when she said: "I wish that you wouldn't kill me, Peter. It would disappoint Eddie. It would disappoint my father."

Peter shrugged. "We can't change who we are, can we? No, we cannot. I was born to live and you were born to die, my beautiful Bryony." He coughed. "This wind, it's blowing sand in my face. However do you get used to it? I can't breathe."

"Just give yourself a little while, for it is unsettled now. It anticipates the rain, and they do not get along. The sand is fighting but soon it will lose, at least for a while."

The rain, emboldened by her confidence, pounded itself to the earth. Peter groaned.

"This is unlike anything that I have ever seen. It almost makes me want to rush the killing process, but I won't, because you're special, Bryony, and you've waited for me just as I have waited for you. I won't hurry it, because that wouldn't be fair to either of us. I want you to be happy and free, and to think of me fondly as you die. I almost lost you to that idiot on the trail, and I sent you gifts, like the star pendant on the body you found in the water. You missed the necklace, didn't you? That's okay, I'm not mad at you, so please don't worry about it. And I sent you all of those flowers, and I got rid of that fishy man at the market who was always annoying you. Do you see how much I have done for you?" He smiled. How kind and benevolent of him. He blinked the rain out of his eyes and pressed his lips to her wet hair.

Bryony went still, then.

When she spoke, her voice sounded strange, unfamiliar, as if the ghost inside of her had risen up and taken over while the real Bryony sank to the floor to catch her breath. It took on the sound of the rain.

"Chad? Are you saying you hurt my Chad?"

Lightning struck somewhere on the far off mesa, and Bryony reflexively threw her arms over her head. The stars on her wrist glittered.

Peter stepped around so he faced her, his hands still in her hair. "Oh, my little Star Girl, are you ready to go back home?" He showed her his knife, and Bryony's reaction startled him.

"Peter Culpert, you put that knife down and let me go, do you hear me? I am not for you! Didn't you hear what my father said? I am not for you!"

And suddenly she was thrashing, kicking and punching unlike anything he had ever seen. Her hair flung water into his face and she threw her body at him. Surprised, he loosened his grip on the knife and she knocked it cleanly from his hand.

She wanted to live. She wanted to live. She was going to fight like she ought to fight, like the women used to fight way back when. She didn't read the magazines; she didn't subscribe to the television shows. She was going to give it her all, and although beaten and bruised with blood coursing down her face from the burst stitches, Bryony Adams was going to go down swinging.

What joy! What delight! His little bird wasn't going to disappoint him after all.

Peter threw his head back and laughed.

Chapter Fifty Nine
Blood and Wind and Rain

There comes a time in everyone's life when a decision must be made.

There are always decisions being made, every second of every day, and sometimes that decision is simply not to decide. However, it needs be said that one day every living thing on this earth will make The Utmost Decision, the decision that will change the rest of their existence one way or the other. What is this decision, you ask? It is different for everybody, and you will not know what yours will be until the time comes, and perhaps even then you will not realize the importance of your choice.

But as for our dear Bryony, when the time came and she was faced with her Utmost Decision, she realized the ramification of that instant with serene clarity. In fact, as she stood there in the blood and wind and rain with a killer and his brightly shining knife, the terror subsided for a perfect moment and she had amazing presence of mind.

She thought, "He has found me, and I am caught. It is time."

213

She thought, "I will never see my husband again. I will never see my friends or the flower shop. How very disheartening."

She thought, "How I long to live. I want to live."

And that was it.

The magic words: "I want to live."

Not a difficult thing to understand, not really. Not an unachievable desire, not too much to ask for. She wanted what others were fortunate enough to take for granted. She wanted a future. She wanted a life, things to look forward to. Despite everything thrown at her, despite what had been ripped away, she planted her feet firmly in the desert sand and challenged fate, challenged the universe. It was as if the cosmos stopped, and fate blinked its eyes quickly.

What, Bryony wanted to survive, really? Could her will be as strong as the will of the universe? Should she get a sporting chance? She wanted to live.

So, if one wants something very, very much, then what does one do to achieve it? One fights, of course.

And fight she did, everything Rikki-Tikki ever taught her, everything they carefully practiced in her living room, and everything she practiced on her own. She ripped away from Peter, leaving a handful of hair in his hand, and threw a left hook and some amazingly well-placed jabs, and an uppercut, and a few roundhouse kicks. When she knocked the knife to the ground, she felt a small thrill of victory, but only for a few seconds, because there was still fear. There was also still anger, so much anger. And when the killer started laughing, her anger only rose until she turned into a beautiful nuclear holocaust. He had no right. She was not meant for him.

Bryony threw herself to the ground, scrabbling for the knife. The torrential rain hit hard between her shoulder blades. It ran down the back of her neck and alarmed her with its brazenness, the way it sought out the vulnerable areas of her body—behind her ears, in the crooks of her elbows—without her permission. Never, never again without her permission. It was her life, her body, her soul. The ghosts of herself billowed around her with the clouds. She couldn't see the knife through the rain, couldn't feel it in the frozen mud.

Peter's laughter mixed with the shrieking of the wind, and it galvanized her. They had become one and the same, a desert of terrors, and she refused to lie down and lift her throat to the knife. She deserved this life.

Bryony saw a faint glimmer in the mud, and reached for it.

Peter kicked her out of the way so hard she slid in the mud. She clutched at her side in agony but then crawled back. The mud was freezing, a grudging mix of hateful sand and rain, and it sucked at her strength.

Peter bent down for the knife.

"No!" Bryony screamed, and threw herself at him, wrapping her arms around his knees. He slipped and went down, and Bryony was past him in seconds. The ground couldn't soak up any more water, and it was starting to stand in the divots pushed up by their feet. Lightning struck closer, hitting the bare ground atop another mesa. There was nothing out here to protect them, nothing to shield them from the lightning. When it moved away from the mesa, she and Peter would be the tallest things in the desert. Stop had warned her about this, had taught her not to make herself a target, but how could she avoid it when she needed to flee for her life? How?

Bryony grabbed the knife at the wrong end, and the blade sunk deep into her frozen fingers. She flipped the knife around, ignoring the blood that dripped from her hand and fed itself to the mud. The anxious, hungry mewing sound of the desert made Bryony's stomach turn.

I am not for you, she thought, and slowly got to her feet. She held the knife on Peter.

"Let me go, Peter. Or I will kill you, I swear I will. Neither of us has to die."

Peter pulled himself to his knees. He was covered in mud and his hair was plastered by the rain, which ran in rivulets across the ground. His eyes were wild with need, a kind of desire Bryony had never seen. For the first time he looked like a monster to her, not the imaginary monsters that appear in stories with faeries and witches, but the kind you run into at a bank, and then they ask you out for coffee, and then a movie, and after a few weeks of this, you trust them enough to invite them over for dinner. And when you are lining your mouth with red and slipping especially pretty shoes onto your feet, they are donning rubber gloves and making sure everything is ready. After he is temporarily satiated, he then boxes up what he loves best about you—your lovely ring finger, for example, or that fine part of the unusually high and delicate arch on your foot—and wraps them away for himself as a lovely gift to open later.

"You want me," Bryony said, and the realization of it nearly made her crumble. The power of that wanting was devastatingly strong, and she felt the weight of it on her slender shoulders, beating on her back like the rain. She took a step back and splashed in the water that was now almost to her ankles. The wind rippled it and pushed it downhill with aggression. Bryony saw something wriggling wash by. It was beginning.

Peter laughed again, but his eyes were on her and they were dark, nailing her to different pieces of wood in his mind. "Of course I want you. I want you more than anybody ever has, not even your husband. How does that make you feel, Bryony? I need you, I crave you. I know how the desert has been feeling all of these years. I am going to have you, do you understand? I am going to knock you to the ground and hold your face in the mud and water until you stop fighting. Do you have any idea how that will feel? For both of us? I will stroke your hair as you die, and tell you that you fulfill me, that your death somehow makes my life complete. I will kiss your face and your hair in gratitude, and then I will take that knife you're holding on me so shakily, so clumsily, and I will show you how it is done."

He slowly stood up, and Bryony twitched the knife in his direction, but her throat went sour. She blinked water out of her eyes and realized there were tears, as well.

"Don't make me hurt you, Peter," she said. Her voice wavered, so she tried to make it strong. "Please don't make me use this on you. I don't want to, but I will."

Peter took a slow step forward, and red ran across Bryony's vision. She would have to slash, to tear, she would go for his face or his chest, and it would pull against his skin, ripping, and the blood would flow.

She knew how it would be, hadn't she lived through it herself? Feeling her skin shred. Feeling it flay and fall away, her life leaking out, everything she had fought so hard for, everything she had tried so hard to save. She had spent her entire fragile existence running, and for what? To have her tender skin slashed to ribbons? Could she really do that to another human being? Could she stand so close to him and cause him the same panic she had felt herself? She pictured the gash across his face in her mind, and gasped.

She couldn't do it. It made her faint to think of it, imagining the look that would cross Peter's face. The agonized look of surprised betrayal.

Peter saw this immediately, and he smiled. "Give me the knife, Bryony. It is a burden to you, but to me it is a joy. There is nothing like feeling metal puncture the flesh, sliding through the fat and moving under the skin. It's . . . like heaven. It's worth the time, worth the effort of stalking and attacking and hiding. I could flay myself off a nice little patch, couldn't I? I could cut myself a lock of your hair and keep it forever. I could remove your pale gray eyes and keep them near me. It's not such a bad thing, really. You will be with me forever. You will be the standard to which I hold up every other woman, every other kill. Others will forget you. You will fade in their minds until they only remember what they choose to remember. They'll forget the weight of your impending death and the weariness that nearly crushes you, but me? I will remember you wholly. It's love, my sweet one. Yes, it's a different love than you have ever known, but it is love all the same, and dare I say it? It is a truer and purer love than you have ever experienced. Look at your husband. Look at your father. Look at how they have left you. But have I left you? No."

He took another step closer, and Bryony trembled. She did not lunge at him with the knife. She did not turn and bound away. The water rushed faster past her feet, tugging at her with desperate urgency, trying to pull her to the ground.

"Yes," it told her. "Give him the knife. Let him do what everybody wishes. I will have you, he will have you, and you will be truly loved. He accepts you, not in spite of who you are, but exactly for who you are. Isn't that what you always wanted? He will remember you after you're gone."

Peter reached out his hand. "Who is here with you at your last moments, my beautiful Star Girl? Who is here? It is me. It is me. It is me."

The thunder roared, battling the sound of the wind for dominance. Peter's words were caught in the noise, tossed in it like the tiny skeleton of a bird, ripped apart and put back together in haphazard and grotesque ways. The wriggling around their feet had grown intense. Rattlesnakes, scorpions. Habitants of the desert panicked from being driven out of their homes. Badgers and mice cringing from the lightning that lit the sky. Bryony's hair crackled on the back of her neck despite the weight of the water.

"Peter," she said softly. He was still approaching her as though she were a beaten animal. He was so careful not to spook her, moving slowly, speaking gently. There was a loud crack and lightning flashed again, illuminating his face, but not his eyes. Somehow they seemed to illuminate themselves.

"What, Bryony?" he asked, and reached for the knife. His eyes sparked.

"I'm sorry," she said, and plunged the knife into his shoulder, deliberately missing his heart. He screamed and grabbed at the wound, but she had already pulled the knife out and hurled it as far as she could into the darkness. She smacked at his bloody shoulder with her fist, and as he doubled over, she kicked him hard in the head, sending him down into the water. Then she turned and ran.

Her feet splashed through the flooded desert, and they cried: "Victory! Victory! Life!" She didn't dare look over her shoulder. She didn't have the time. She ran, zipping through the water as though she were skating on top of it. The euphoria almost made her think she was.

She heard shrieking behind her, and tried to block it out. Perhaps it was the wind, that ever mischievous wind, making sounds that would ordinarily entice her gentle heart to go back and see if somebody needed help. For they were, you see, screams of the most horrible kind, the type of screaming that makes one shudder and wish they had never heard them, for now they will lie awake at night thinking about the tragedy that befell the screamer. And not one night, but many, many nights, for there is a shame inside when one doesn't help another, and it grows into an all-consuming worm. It is fairly easy to identify who suffers from this worm; they are always wrapped in blankets and warm cable knit sweaters to shield themselves from the cold, because they don't deserve to feel the sun, they don't deserve for their blood to run comfortably at a nice, predictable temperature. They are the ones who let somebody die, they heard the screams and never looked, never helped, and therefore gave up their chance at being a Real Person. Now they are an unfortunate ghost, a lost phantom.

But Bryony had been a ghost since before she was born. She was the girl who was born to die, and so never really lived, even though she had certainly tried. She would ignore these screams, and Peter, and would send the police to look for him later, which was rather kind of her, considering. But that might be useless, because she knew exactly what was happening to him.

He was being punished for letting her go.

The frightened, creeping things of the desert had found Peter. They were clinging to him with their claws and teeth and stingers. They wrapped their thorns and vines around him, climbing over him, burrowing beneath him. He tried to crawl through the muddy water that had turned into a small river, the dreaded flash flood desert dwellers are warned of. The desert fed itself to him in the form of mud and running water that washed over him, through him, covering him with fur and scales and debris. The ground would find marrow to satiate its craving after all, and if it wasn't going to be the Star Girl's, then it would certainly be he who was chosen to murder her and failed.

The screams increased in pitch and then were cut off, and the desert made a sound that nearly stopped Bryony in her tracks, so full of revulsion and disgust was she. The awfulness! But her desire was strong, and so were her legs, and so was her spirit. She wasn't clear yet, but she would make it, she would make it, she would live.

Suddenly the sky illuminated as though a meteor crashed to the earth, as though it was the atomic bomb all over again. Thunder, so loud, so close and monstrous that she screamed and threw her arms over her head to stave off the lightning blooming and blossoming in front of her eyes like her beloved yellow jonquils, and it was too much, she had come so far, but there are always more tricks to be pulled from somebody's sleeve, and this last one was the cruelest of all, and our Star Girl fell to the ground like a star from the sky from whence she came, and there her broken heart stopped.

Chapter Sixty
The End

Oh, what a terrible story!

How could it be that we followed Bryony's journey from the time she was a little girl, ignorant of all that would befall her, through her first kiss and college and meeting friends and Eddie and her tormented killer and her fight to the death, and then she dies in the end?

She dies. Bryony falls to the ground like a flower, and we are left to mourn her. More than that, we feel betrayed. We invested time and interest. We cheered her on and we shouted: "No, don't let that man in your home!" and "Eddie, what are you doing, you must go with Bryony!" and "Hooray, Teddy Baker, you had decency inside of you all along, and we are so very proud of you for your choices!" Perhaps there were even a few thoughts of, "I wonder what a jonquil looks like. I shall certainly run to look one up and educate myself so I may better relate to the tale of Bryony and her Eddie."

Perhaps you are angry, dear reader. Perhaps you hoped better for our girl, because she was so genuine and caring, and a good person deserves good things. Perhaps you are frustrated with the narrator and are thinking to yourself: "I would have told a much better story, and the ending would have been satisfying. There would have been hot air balloons and sunshine and confetti that fell from the sky. Most importantly, she would have lived. For I know what makes a good story, and it is only a good story when the end wraps itself up nicely and neatly and adorns itself with a bow."

You must know this: There are not always happy endings. Wouldn't it be wonderful if this was true? Unfortunately, it is not.

"But it isn't fair!" you cry.

Yes, you are absolutely right, but life was not meant to be fair, it was meant to be lived.

Despite the smudge of impending doom that hung over her, did our Bryony not try to live? Did she not hold her friends close to her? Did she not throw her arms around Chad the Fish Guy, and speak to the old woman who sells peaches at the market, and laugh with Syrina as they packed for her spontaneous wedding, and generally enjoy the wonders life gave her? There was sorrow and sweetness and pain and joy. Did she not choose joy? As with all tales, this one has a moral, and the moral is this: Live.

And yet . . .

And yet, this is also an amazing universe, rife with beauty and surprises.

Never forget that.

Even as you mourn, my tender-hearted reader, remember this: Never give up hope.

Chapter Sixty One
There Is No End

Lightning did not hit our sweet Bryony. The same time it flashed, a car came spinning out of nowhere, and its headlights were stark and bright and almost blinded our dear girl. Her heart shivered and stopped momentarily, quite knocked out of sorts by the extreme overload, but soon came back to itself and began to beat resolutely.

Car doors slammed and feet hurried over to her.

"Bryony!" cried out a voice, a familiar voice, a dear and good voice. Bryony raised her head and looked through the veil of water to see death had been kind enough to send her an angel who looked, sounded, and, oh my, felt just like her Eddie.

"Bryony, I will never leave you again, I swear it. Never, never," he said, and buried his face into her wet hair, and kissed her cold face and lips and cheeks and fingers. He gently caressed her burst stitches and tried not to cry.

A man walked up from behind him and held out a blanket. Eddie helped Bryony to her feet and she was soon wrapped head to toe in warm softness.

"Hello, Bryony," said Detective Bridger. He smiled at her, and something about his endearingly crooked front tooth made her lips pull up slightly in response. "I am very pleased to see you alive and quite literally all in one piece. I was afraid we would be too late."

He opened the car door for her, bowing like a gentleman. Eddie helped Bryony inside, and then slid in after her.

"Where is Peter?" he asked her. His eyes were angry but his voice was soft, and Bryony was happy, and tired, and overwhelmed, and still couldn't believe her husband had suddenly shown up out in the middle of nowhere like somebody out of a dream.

"Sing me a song, Eddie. Please? Something beautiful that doesn't have anything to do with death." For dreams cannot sing, at least, not here in the real waking world, and if this man opened his mouth and words and music poured out, then she would know it was her love, her best friend, her quirky and irritable and inordinately wonderful Eddie.

Eddie arched an eyebrow at her, but her face pleaded and her eyes were without shine, and he would have given her anything at all, and a song would be a pleasure. He didn't have Jasmine the Guitar, but he sang the lovely ballad he composed just for his wife, the song she had never heard. Then he was silent.

"It really is you," she said, and rested her head against his shoulder. She closed her eyes and sighed. "I have missed you so much. It has been a terrible time . . . "

She couldn't say anything more, and it was to be expected. Eddie kissed her fiercely and said: "I am sorry, Bryony. I wish more than anything I could have come here with you. I thought sending Peter to watch over you was better than you going alone, but I was so very wrong."

Bryony looked at him with her wan gray eyes. She was tired, and it seemed too much effort to blink, to see, and even though she was safe now and warming up nicely, everything still faded away in front of her vision until she saw nothing at all.

"Why didn't you come, Eddie? Is your career so important?" It was raining inside of the car now, water coursing from her eyes and then her clothes and hair as Eddie threw his arms around her.

"No, of course not. It was never the career. It was something else, something I was too ashamed to tell you, but I should have and I'm sorry, and I will always tell the truth from now on because it will make things so much easier. Bryony, I have been recording, and I've been at the station, and practicing, of course, but that isn't where I have been spending the majority of my time. I . . . I have been with this detective here, day and night, and during the course of this time he and I—"

"You two were having an *affair*?!" she demanded.

Eddie's mouth dropped open, and Detective Bridger laughed.

"I was investigating him for murder," he assured Bryony. "Several murders, actually," and then he laughed some more.

"Oh. Well that is perfectly all right, then," she said, and kissed Eddie. "If that is all it was, why didn't you just tell me?"

"Murder, Bryony. They thought I had killed all of those women, and I had ties to them. The woman missing from the market and the woman from the bookstore I play at on Thursday nights. And of course Rita and my mother, and the body you found. She was dating this guy I know named Mike, and really he was a terrible loser. It doesn't change the fact that it was like a web of bodies, and it seemed as though I was connected to them somehow, and it was a horrible, thing. I didn't want to tell you, because I was so angry, and I didn't want you to think poorly of me. So I was under investigation, and was forbidden to leave the area, which is why I couldn't go. But something was wrong, and I stormed into the detective's office and told him I had sent you home to see your father and this man named Peter Culpert had gone with you, and it wasn't right. It should have been *me*. And I said they could arrest me as soon as I came back, but I had to go find you. I could feel it. Death was so close to you, I could smell it on your breath as you slept. It was time."

Detective Bridger met Bryony's eyes in the rearview mirror. "I didn't believe Eddie had done it, personally, but he was close to an awful lot of the victims."

"That's because they were close to me," she said rather fiercely, and raised her chin to give the detective what she hoped was a stern and chastising glance. Eddie the Murderer, indeed.

Detective Bridger grinned. "Right, but when he said the name Peter Culpert, the alarms rang in my head. I had been looking into him, myself. He told us that he had chased your attacker off the trail, but there was so much blood, and Peter was covered in it. He looked so calm when we got to him, sitting quietly in a pool of crimson, completely unfazed. Seeing you lying in his lap while he blinked at me with blood running down his face, it just . . . Then we came across a body, and it matched the DNA we found all over Peter. Why would he say he scared the guy off when he had actually killed him? So I told Eddie he could find you, but only if I could come. Where is Peter, anyway?"

Bryony looked out of the window at the storming sky. The munching sounds were undeniable, and quite disturbing, but far off she could see a place where the clouds had opened up, and a few stars peeped out tentatively.

"He belongs to the desert now," she said, and the car was silent except for the sound of the rain and the gallantry of the windshield wipers.

Nothing was said, and although Detective Bridger didn't completely understand the situation, he was not immune to the archaic and devious murmurings the desert made. He vowed to search for the remains of Peter Culpert in the morning, but not until the sun came out. Deep within all of us swims a primal fear of the dark and the stealthy creatures that inhabit it, and no matter how polished and mature and respected we become, when we are alone and it is quiet, the ancient things of the night whisper to us that they are there, and we are quite defenseless. We are no match for the evils so much older than we.

"Yes, the morning will be fine," Eddie said to the detective as if he had spoken aloud, and he reached forward to pat his shoulder.

"Right then," Detective Bridger said, and was grateful.

And thus it was.

They held Stop's funeral a few days later. The mud had already dried and hardened, and Bryony managed to smile as they lowered his casket into the ground. She stood beside Eddie and Syrina and Rikki-Tikki, and Teddy, his wife, and their baby, and all of her friends and neighbors she had grown up with.

Bryony was holding a particularly stunning bouquet of fresh flowers from her little stand at the market. They were yellow and purple and red, and full of happiness and joy and the "We wish you well!" and "Come home soon!" sentiments from those back home who missed her. She glanced over her shoulder at Syrina, who was giving her the thumbs up.

"I held those flowers the entire flight," Syrina whispered to the butcher beside her. "Bryony is especially fond of yellow jonquils, you know." She was extremely proud of herself, and had every right to be, for although she sneezed a bit during the flight, she refused to let Rikki-Tikki take the flowers from her at all, and it was a labor of love that did not go unappreciated.

"Thank you!" Bryony had cried, throwing her arms around Syrina. The flowers were nearly knocked loose, and Eddie stepped in quickly to save them.

"You're welcome!" Syrina answered back, throwing her arms around Bryony.

"I love you," Bryony said, and wiped her eyes.

"I love you, too." Syrina cried without any shame whatsoever, and they looked at the flowers and the clouds and each other.

Bryony had never had a sister, but she had one now, and they would never be parted for the remainder of their days, although they did not yet know this. But you, dear reader, are privileged enough to have a brief glimpse of the future, and know this: The future is lovely, and it is spectacular, and it is full of happy things for Bryony and the good friends who have become her family.

"'Sup?" Rikki-Tikki had said to Eddie, and they clapped each other firmly on their backs, and their smiles were wide and as bright as the sky.

Bryony took a step forward. She tucked one of the flowers behind her ear, and tossed the rest onto her father's casket. They fell soft, bright, and beautiful. The casket became a marvel, and it was exactly as it should be.

"I love you, Daddy. Now you are free and can go wherever you want without being chained to this desert. It has no hold on either of us anymore. I do hope you check in on me from time to time. I think Eddie and I are going to be very happy together."

Eddie took her hand, and it flashed and glittered and shone. Bryony had decorated it with a delicate yet surprisingly resilient bracelet made of silver stars.

Oliver Bloom
by Ryan Johnson

1

Oliver Bloom was born the day his father died, but an hour after. When it was finished and the doctor handed Emily Bloom her son, fresh and new, the joy in her tears mixed with loss, and she knew the worst was over.

2

The Bloom family had never been rich, or had the greenest lawn or the freshest paint on their house, but those who knew them knew, without mistake, that Emily Bloom enjoyed the finest entertainment in town—nightly and for free—at the hands of her husband and his guitar.

When Emily returned home from the hospital, child in arm, and flipped on the lights, it was that beat-up guitar leaning against the couch that made her knees wobble and her eyes burn. She went to the baby's room—the one she and her husband had spent so many hours preparing, filling with all the laughter and hope they could muster. She swung open the door and placed the baby in the crib they'd toiled to put together and lacquered in excitement.

She left him there to sleep.

She went back downstairs, sat beside the orphaned guitar too afraid to touch the strings, and make it sing painful reminders. She dragged her fingers along the headstock and picked it up carefully, same as the baby.

She locked it away in the back of the closet.

3

Eleven years and eleven days later, while Oliver was amidst a perilous expedition for hidden Christmas presents his mother surely possessed, he came across an old guitar.

From that day forth, Oliver Bloom was the boy who saw life in eighth notes.

4

Oliver played and performed, performed and played, and practiced in between. His fingers bled, they calloused, but through the pain and peeling skin, notes began holding longer, bent further. Melodies gained complexity, and rhythm became nighttime ocean waves bombarded by falling stars.

Beauty, Oliver learned in his room in the night, came after a little bit of ugly.

And sometimes, there just had to be blood.

5

So years in Oliver Bloom's life passed, through middle school where he spoke with few, to high school, where he spoke to no one.

At lunch he took the money his mother gave him and shoved it into the vending machine, punched the button for the same drink he always had. After that he sat up against the same machine, unconvinced by the sticker warning people died every year when they fell over, and set out on whatever new tune he dreamt of the night before.

In class he couldn't practice, so he begrudgingly suffered through endless lectures, slideshows, and pop quizzes. He never studied. He never had to. School came naturally, and he was grateful; studying would have adversely affected his more creative exploits.

Days blurred together for Oliver most months—until a fortuitous event occurred: a student moved away, leaving an opening in Music Theory class. Hearing the news he went to the counselor, made a case for himself to be transferred into the newly available seat. He told the cold-faced, bespectacled woman how he languished in French II, how his talents and future would be much behooved by the simple mashing of a few computer keys, freeing him from archaic, uninteresting European culture and thrusting him full speed into the colorful world of academic bliss.

The counselor eventually agreed. With a keystroke, Oliver Bloom's high school life changed forever.

6

It didn't happen right away like in the movies, when he walked into class with his guitar slung over his back. Without fanfare he surveyed the room, probably glanced over her once or twice without even noticing. The only empty seat beckoned. He took it and sighed, set down his pack and his father's guitar.

The teacher walked into class and wasted no time beginning the day's lesson.

Oliver scribbled notes over the next fifty minutes and understood every word. He wrote melody lines in the margins for fun, and when the teacher walked by, he watched Oliver, nodding. Not impressed, but approving.

The bell rang. Oliver gathered his things.

He saw her.

Half notes swirled in his stomach; a bass clef stuck in his throat.

She glowed, but she didn't really. She floated, but she didn't really. Her hair danced while she walked, and it shone.

She was a girl.

No, she was a star—like from outer space. Not the kind in movies.

Oliver gulped down the sensation of drowning. He sat back in his desk, pretended to fumble through his pack for some nonexistent item he desperately needed— anything to make sure she didn't leave before she—

She left.

Oliver stood, bewildered by the other students, making sure each had been blinded like him.

No one else had noticed.

7

Oliver was wrong; another boy had indeed noticed, and was already several steps ahead.

8

Oliver had never been a large child, but never a small one either; he was just the right size for a boy with no ambition to participate in activities where brute strength was a factor. This should be noted for later.

9

It was another week before Oliver finally gathered his courage and sat next to her. "Hi," he almost whispered.

"Hello," replied the girl.

"I'm Oliver."

"Hello, Olly."

"Oliver."

"It's very nice to meet you, Olly," the girl replied with a surprising amount of terseness.

Oliver frowned, dug his pencil into his desk. "Well? What's *your* name?"

The girl leafed through some papers, didn't bother looking at him when she answered, "Why would you want to know that?"

Oliver blinked. Did people really ask questions like that? He'd figured out girls were weird. *This* was different.

But her eyes—they were worth some weird. He kept on. "Why wouldn't I?"

"There are reasons not to want to know me."

Oliver flashed the most dashing smile he could. "I can't imagine one."

"Oh?" sighed the girl, and she stopped leafing through those papers long enough to look at him.

Oliver's heart froze. There was that feeling again: She wasn't a girl, she was more than that. She'd be the reason he'd do something incredible, or at least something stupid. There was a sadness in her face he couldn't quite put his finger on, and it made him instantly angry, like he wanted to punch whatever was responsible.

He opened his mouth to say more—the bell cut him off. The girl's attention snapped to the front of class.

Oliver clenched his teeth and gave up. "I'll write you a song!" he almost yelled.

She turned, smiled.

It was something. It was a start.

10

Months passed, and somewhere between lectures the Star Girl spoke up, without prompting on Oliver's part—a new development. "Will you be attending the party Friday night? The one at Teddy's?"

Oliver rolled his eyes. "No."

"I am," she said in a voice like a swirl of colors.

"So am I. Totally."

11

Oliver hated parties, and not for the obvious reasons: He didn't think he was better than the others, or smarter, or destined for greater things. Boredom, on the other hand—it weighed upon him. Parties were terrible. And boring.

So boring.

That night classmates got drunk and Oliver watched it happen. They kissed people they wouldn't want anyone else knowing about the next morning. Terrible music blasted from the hands of a first-time DJ fancying himself a pro.

"This party sucks!" Oliver said, louder than he meant to.

"Of course it does!" replied Donavon Clemons, grabbing on to Oliver's arm. "Boring, right? Come on, follow me."

Oliver begrudgingly followed to the driveway. A half dozen boys stood gathered around the car parked there. It must have had an impressive engine, or paint job, or something. Oliver had no idea. It was loud when the key in it turned.

"Oliver!" Teddy Baker called. He barely looked at him and added, "Didn't think you'd be around."

"Hey, Teddy."

"Good party? Having fun?"

"Sure, I mean—"

"Hot girls all over the place, right?"

"I guess."

Teddy flipped off the stereo, popped out from the driver's side. "It sucks."

"Yeah."

"I know," nodded Teddy. "Things'll get interesting. We're gonna kill her. Tonight."

"Kill her?"

"Bryony."

He didn't have to say the name. Oliver already knew. "They'll catch you. You and your friends."

Teddy nodded, "Sure they will, but why's that matter? Killing a girl meant to be killed. We did a service, you know? Now no one else has to bother with it. We're heroes—taking one for the team."

The other boys smiled, nodded at each other in ways that turned Oliver's stomach.

"She *likes* you, Teddy," said Oliver.

"Even easier, then."

"No, I mean, she *really* likes you. Like, you could date her. She'd—"

"*Come on*, Oliver," sighed Teddy.

Oliver shook his head, let out a sigh of his own. "Where's it gonna happen?"

Then Teddy smiled. "The desert. The Dead Rocks. Make it a spectacle, you know? Like a movie."

"Like a movie," repeated Oliver. "She trusts me."

"Yep."

"She'll go if I take her."

"That's what me and the guys were thinking."

Oliver scanned over the group, saw it in their eyes that they'd killed her already. He took a breath. "Yeah, ok. I'll see you guys out there. The Dead Rocks?"

"The Dead Rocks."

12

It wasn't hard, luring Bryony. "Teddy Baker will be there," Oliver told her. "Said he wants to ask you something."

"About . . . the dance?" Her excitement was painful, beautiful the way it burst.

Star Girl.

"That's the rumor," Oliver half-smiled. He held open the car door, waved her in.

And like that, they were off to the murder.

13

It was a mistake, stopping too close to the Dead Rocks.

"Oh, look!" The Star Girl gasped. "Do you really think—"

"Quiet!" Oliver snapped back.

She asked three questions that night.

"Why are they carrying sheets?"

Oliver shrugged, bit his tongue. "Making banners, I'd guess. Teddy said he was gonna make it like a movie. Asking you to the dance, I mean."

"And shovels?"

Oliver cleared his throat. "Heard of the Nazca lines? Things you can't see until you're way up high? Like, in a helicopter high. Teddy said he wanted to ask you there *big*. Maybe something like that?"

The Star Girl nodded, understanding.

"What about those barrels? And the fire?"

"Fireworks," replied Oliver, and even he was surprised at how natural the lie came out.

"Oh."

Lies were heavy, Oliver learned. They stacked upon each other, until Oliver did the only thing he knew how.

"Wait here," Oliver said.

He got out of the car.

14

"Hey, Teddy."

"Olly, what's up? Where's Bryony?"

"Back in the car. She thinks you're gonna ask her to the dance."

"Classic! We're almost ready, so get her, huh?"

"Yeah. About that."

Sometimes there just had to be blood, and Oliver swung with every ounce. His fist connected with Teddy's face. He felt his knuckles crack; a vision-blurring spark of pain shot up his arm.

A second swing; Oliver didn't feel anything at all.

The third swing Teddy's jaw gave way.

"Speak to her again! Say a word to her again! See what happens!" Oliver screamed in Teddy Baker's bleeding ear.

After that Oliver swung in eighth notes. He lost count how many times.

15

Someone told.

The suspension was supposed to last three days - just the right amount of time for Oliver to finish the song he promised her.

On the third day, he received a letter from school.

Apparently, Teddy Baker's father wasn't happy with the way his son's face looked and he'd made a ruckus.

Apparently, that was enough.

Oliver's three-day suspension became permanent expulsion.

Oliver changed schools, to one where they didn't have music classes.

He never saw the Star Girl again.

16

Oliver grew older; he wondered if she was still alive.

He thought she probably was.

The end?

Not if you dive into Mercedes' other books:

Nameless: The Darkness Comes—Luna Masterson sees demons. She has been dealing with the demonic all her life, so when her brother gets tangled up with a demon named Sparkles, 'Luna the Lunatic' rolls in on her motorcycle to save the day. Armed with the ability to harm demons, her scathing sarcasm, and a hefty chip on her shoulder, Luna gathers the most unusual of allies, teaming up with a green-eyed heroin addict and a snarky demon 'of some import.' After all, outcasts of a feather should stick together . . . even until the end.

Little Dead Red—The Wolf is roaming the city, and he must be stopped. In this modern day retelling of Little Red Riding Hood, the wolf takes to the city streets to capture his prey, but the hunter is close behind him. With Grim Marie on the prowl, the hunter becomes the hunted.

Apocalyptic Montessa and Nuclear Lulu: A Tale of Atomic Love—Montessa Tovar is walking home alone when she is abducted by Lu, a serial killer with unusual talents and a grudge against the world. But in time, the victim becomes the executioner as 'Aplocalyptic' Montessa and her doomed 'Nuclear' Lulu crisscross the country in a bloody firestorm of revenge. HER MAMA ALWAYS SAID SHE WAS SPECIAL. HIS DADDY CALLED HIM A DEMON. BUT EVEN MONSTERS CAN FALL IN LOVE.

If you enjoyed this book, I'm sure you'll also like the following titles:

Wind Chill by Patrick Rutigliano—What if you were held captive by your own family? Emma Rawlins has spent the last year a prisoner. The months following her mother's death dragged her father into a paranoid spiral of conspiracy theories and doomsday premonitions. But there is a force far colder than the freezing drifts. Ancient, ravenous, it knows no mercy. And it's already had a taste . . .

Tales from The Lake Vol.1 anthology—Remember those dark and scary nights spent telling ghost stories and other campfire stories? With the *Tales from The Lake* horror anthologies, you can relive some of those memories by reading the best Dark Fiction stories around. Includes Dark Fiction stories and poems by horror greats such as Graham Masterton, Bev Vincent, Tim Curran, Tim Waggoner, Elizabeth Massie, and many more. Be sure to check out our website for future *Tales from The Lake* volumes.

Flowers in a Dumpster by Mark Allan Gunnells—The world is full of beauty and mystery. In these 17 tales, Gunnells will take you on a journey through landscapes of light and darkness, rapture and agony, hope and fear. Let Gunnells guide you through these landscapes where magnificence and decay co-exist side by side. Come pick a bouquet from these Flowers in a Dumpster.

Eidolon Avenue: The First Feast by Jonathan Winn—where the secretly guilty go to die. All thrown into their own private hell as every cruel choice, every deadly mistake, every drop of spilled blood is remembered, resurrected and relived to feed the ancient evil that lives on Eidolon Avenue.

Through a Mirror, Darkly by Kevin Lucia—Are there truths within the books we read? What if the book delves into the lives of the very town you live in? People you know? Or thought you knew. These are the questions a bookstore owner face when a mysterious book shows up.

Samurai and Other Stories by William Meikle—No one can handle Scottish folklore with elements of the darkest horror, science fiction and fantasy, suspense and adventure like William Meikle.

The Dark at the End of the Tunnel by Taylor Grant— Offered for the first time in a collected format, this selection features ten gripping and darkly imaginative stories by Taylor Grant, a Bram Stoker Award® nominated author and rising star in the suspense and horror genres. Grant exposes the terrors that hide beneath the surface of our ordinary world, behind people's masks of normalcy, and lurking in the shadows at the farthest reaches of the universe.

If you ever thought of becoming an author, I'd also like to recommend these non-fiction titles:

The *Writers On Writing: An Author's Guide* Series— Your favorite authors share their secrets in the ultimate guide to becoming and being and author. With your support, *Writers On Writing* will become an ongoing eBook series with original 'On Writing' essays by writing professionals. A new edition will be launched every few months, featuring four or five essays per edition, so be sure to check out the webpage regularly for updates.

Horror 101: The Way Forward—a comprehensive overview of the Horror fiction genre and career opportunities available to established and aspiring authors, including Jack Ketchum, Graham Masterton, Edward Lee, Lisa Morton, Ellen Datlow, Ramsey Campbell, and many more.

Horror 201: The Silver Scream Vol.1 and *Vol.2*—A must read for anyone interested in the horror film industry. Includes interviews and essays by Wes Craven, John Carpenter, George A. Romero, Mick Garris, and dozens more. Now available in paperback, as well.

Modern Mythmakers: 35 interviews with Horror and Science Fiction Writers and Filmmakers by Michael McCarty—Ever wanted to hang out with legends like Ray Bradbury, Richard Matheson, and Dean Koontz? *Modern Mythmakers* is your chance to hear fun anecdotes and career advice from authors and filmmakers like Forrest J. Ackerman, Ray Bradbury, Ramsey Campbell, John Carpenter, Dan Curtis, Elvira, Neil Gaiman, Mick Garris, Laurell K. Hamilton, Jack Ketchum, Dean Koontz, Graham Masterton, Richard Matheson, John Russo, William F. Nolan, John Saul, Peter Straub, and many more.

Or check out other Crystal Lake Publishing books for your Dark Fiction, Horror, Suspense, and Thriller needs.

Biography

Mercedes M. Yardley is a dark fantasist who wears stilettos, red lipstick, and poisonous flowers in her hair. She is the author of the short story collection *Beautiful Sorrows,* the novellas *Apocalyptic Montessa and Nuclear Lulu: A Tale of Atomic Love* and *Little Dead Red,* and the novels *Nameless: The Darkness Comes* and *Pretty Little Dead Girls: A Novel of Murder and Whimsy.* She often speaks at conferences and teaches workshops on several subjects, including personal branding and how to write a novel in stolen moments. Mercedes lives and works in Sin City with her family and menagerie of Strange and Unusual Pets. You can reach her at www.abrokenlaptop.com.

Connect with the Author

Website:
http://abrokenlaptop.com/

Facebook:
https://www.facebook.com/Mercedes-M-Yardley-259448987862/?fref=ts

Twitter:
https://twitter.com/mercedesmy

Connect with Crystal Lake Publishing

Website (be sure to sign up for our newsletter):
www.crystallakepub.com

Facebook:
www.facebook.com/Crystallakepublishing

Twitter:
https://twitter.com/crystallakepub

With unmatched success since 2012, Crystal Lake Publishing has quickly become one of the world's leading indie publishers of Mystery, Thriller, and Suspense books with a Dark Fiction edge.

Crystal Lake Publishing puts integrity, honor, and respect at the forefront of our operations.

We strive for each book and outreach program that's launched to not only entertain and touch or comment on issues that affect our readers, but also to strengthen and support the Dark Fiction field and its authors.

Not only do we publish authors who are destined to be legends in the field (and as hardworking as us), but we also look for men and women who care about their readers and fellow human beings. We only publish the very best Dark Fiction and look forward to launching many new careers.

We strive to know each and every one of our readers, while building personal relationships with our authors, reviewers, bloggers, pod-casters, bookstores and libraries.

Crystal Lake Publishing is and will always be a beacon of what passion and dedication, combined with overwhelming teamwork and respect, can accomplish: unique fiction you can't find anywhere else.

We do not just publish books, we present you worlds within your world, doors within your mind, from talented authors who sacrifice so much for a moment of your time.

This is what we believe in. What we stand for. This will be our legacy.

Welcome to Crystal Lake Publishing.

We hope you enjoyed this title. If so, we'd be grateful if you could leave a review on your blog or any of the other websites and outlets open to book reviews. Reviews are like gold to writers and publishers, since word-of-mouth is and will always be the best way to market a great book. And remember to keep an eye out for more of our books.

THANK YOU FOR PURCHASING THIS BOOK

Made in the USA
Lexington, KY
29 June 2017